Rose House

Robert Crandall

ISBN: 978-1-7329814-0-9

ALSO BY ROBERT CRANDALL

Night Winds

ACKNOWLEDGMENTS

Special thanks to my wife, Mary Sue, for her support during the creation of this book and the long hours she spent working on it; and to our son, Rob, for time spent discussing it and his unflagging encouragement. A special thanks to friends who reviewed and commented on this book, particularly Ella Roman.

Any errors or omissions are exclusively mine.

Rose House

Did you ever see something that isn't there?

CHAPTER 1

I was new in the area, transferred down here for a job from up north in Chicago, and living in a small apartment near downtown, in a small town in central Louisiana. I planned to sell the Chicago house and find something around here, but then that depended on how long the divorce took and so far, it kept dragging on. So I rented an apartment until that got settled.

The insurance company I worked for offered me a very nice promotion if I moved south, and it just kind of fell in with other things in my life, or maybe I should say fell out. My wife Clara decided that she wanted a divorce because 'it is the best thing for you.' Apparently I didn't get much say in the matter, regardless of how much I argued.

Since my new job was only a short distance away from my apartment, I started walking to work whenever the weather permitted. Maybe I could finally get myself into shape, maybe not, but it was a start. At first I took the most direct route—left onto

Jardin, then down to Des Plaines and turn right to head for the office about ten blocks away. Not a long walk if the weather is good, but the steamy southern summers would be here before you know it.

The other nice thing about walking was it gave me some quiet time to think, and I needed to do a lot of that. Between the new job, the move and the divorce, a lot of things were up in the air and I needed to settle into a new routine of some kind...or maybe that was wishful thinking. I knew it would be hard to replace the friends Clara and I had in Chicago, particularly Matt and Marta, the next-door neighbors we had been very close with. And I really missed Clara, but at the moment that was out of my control.

It didn't take long for me to get tired of walking past the same shops every day—the bakery with their beignets and cafe au lait which I sampled if I had time in the morning, the Tea Shoppe with its beer signs in the window—someone's goofy idea of a name for a local bar. Didn't stop them from getting business, though. There were always cars out front regardless of the time of day. Who goes into a bar at breakfast time, anyway? I've always wondered. Still, it all reminded me of growing up in New Orleans before Dad moved us north to Chicago.

So I started looking for alternate routes to get a little variety. It was a good way to get to know the area and I expect to be here a long time. Initially I wandered a little farther north, through the older businesses and the start of the residential areas. Small, one- and two-story frame houses with carports, and picture windows on the newer ones, stacked close to each other with narrow walkways on either side. The cars in the driveways were older, typically five- to ten-year old Chevrolets, with the odd Buick or Dodge thrown in for good measure. Nothing fancy, but the yards were nicely mowed, the shrubs trimmed, the houses in good repair.

Farther north it started to change again. Same type of houses, same age, and style, maybe a little smaller, but the lawns were ragged, the houses not kept up as well and the occasional car up on blocks in the back of the driveway.

Then I revised my approach and started walking south instead. At first the neighborhoods were the same, but as I started walking farther the cars changed from Chevrolets, Buicks, and Dodges to Cadillacs, Lincolns, and Acuras. Houses were almost all two stories here, with plenty of space between the homes, larger side yards and gardens, and tall trees providing shade from the summer sun. Some of the gardens in the side yards had benches in among the flower beds and some had a canopy or pergola over the top.

As I wandered farther south, I came across several streets with older brick homes, three stories with slate roofs. Many had columned porches and fancy carved woodwork trimming the roofs out front. The yards here were even larger with deep lots and three-car garages and even a few carriage houses. Beautiful old neighborhood.

I was surprised to come across one of them, near the middle of a block, with waist-high weeds throughout the whole yard and no trees at all. The house was in fair shape, though it had a boarded-up window and the trim paint was peeling in several places; the gutters had weeds growing out of them in spots. On the west side of the house was a glassed-in conservatory with some broken panes in the side wall. Even the iron fence next to the sidewalk was leaning and looked wobbly. I saw some benches scattered around the yard and as I looked, it seemed like flagstone pathways wandered past them, but all the leaves strewn around made it hard to tell what it had once looked like. The basics of the house still seemed solid, but it would take a lot of work to get it back into shape, even if only to sell it.

I had my hand on the fence rail, looking around, thinking about how muggy it was that day, unusual for this early in the year, but this was Louisiana, what could you expect? When I caught a glimpse of her to my left, I looked. I only saw her face and shoulders because of the high weeds, and I remember thinking it was a funny place for a kid to play when such pretty lawns were on either side.

She just stood there near a bench, crying silently, shoulders drooping as if she were totally alone, holding a white rose up against her cheek as if it might be the only important thing in the world to her. She sobbed a few more times, and then looked up.

Her eyes met mine, but there was no recognition there. She stared beyond me at something. I remember thinking that those eyes looked far too old for such a young girl. Then a horn sounded behind me and I glanced away. When I turned back, she was gone. Kids… but it was strange that she got away that fast.

CHAPTER 2

I didn't sleep well that night. I'd doze off and then wake up startled, remembering her eyes. A storm came through about two o'clock bringing a cold front into the area, and I got up to close the windows, but that left it feeling humid. In the morning I had vague memories of tossing and turning and the bed was disheveled.

I made a cup of coffee, strong and black, and stood at the window looking out over the wet parking lot. A few branches were down in some of the neighboring yards, but nothing serious. I was staring out across the street, eyes unfocused and thoughts wandering, when I remembered her face. And then the dreams started coming back, but only in vague snatches. She was in all of them, and we were running from something that we couldn't get away from, but I had no idea what. Dreams are funny like that sometimes. You get bits and pieces and the harder you try to figure it out, the fuzzier it gets.

I moved away from the window, finished my coffee, and headed for the shower, still tired and groggy. At this rate, it was going to be a long day.

I took the short way to work that morning, mostly because the beignets at Anna's Bakery were calling my name. I got my order and settled into one of the little bent iron chairs they have and had just started on my coffee when Roger walked in and saw me. He grabbed some coffee, came over, and sat in the chair across from me.

"Hey, Lou, I see you're starting to find your way around town here… wondered when you'd discover Anna's. Some days half the town shows up here, if you're willing to wait for a couple of hours."

I smiled at him; he was the kind of relaxed guy who always had a ready smile and a good word, though he didn't seem very interested in his job at the office.

"Gotta get breakfast somewhere. It's a lot quicker here than fixing something myself, plus it reminds me of New Orleans when I was a kid."

"I remember you saying something a couple of days ago about growing up in the South. Probably brings back a lot of memories."

I grinned to myself as I rubbed my eyes. "Yeah, a lot of good ones from growing up in this part of the country. Many times I wished we had never moved, but then they didn't ask me."

He chuckled quietly, then his face turned serious. "You feeling okay today? Looks like you're under the weather."

"Yeah, literally. The storm got me up in the middle of the night and I was pretty restless after that. I'll be fine after another dozen of these coffees. You heading into the office today or are you off on appointments?"

"Can't find any good excuses, so I guess I'll go in. Hope the boss doesn't have a heart attack when he sees me this early. By the way, thanks again for helping me out with the Abernathys...I wouldn't have thought of using an annuity quite that way."

"No problem. Hang on for a minute and I'll walk over with you."

Eventually, the coffee kicked in and I made it through the day, but I had a hard time focusing on work. A bright and sunny morning had followed up the storm and I caught myself staring out the window a number of times.

By the time we were closing down, I was more than happy to call it a day. Roger left at the same time and suggested a beer, but I took a rain check on that. I just wanted to get out and walk some more.

We split ways at the Tea Shoppe and I headed west through the business section, thinking about a quiet dinner. As I stopped at the light waiting to cross, I noticed Marie's Flowers across the street. I'd passed there numerous times but never paid any attention, so when the light changed, I crossed over and walked in to look around, not really sure what I was looking for.

"Can I help you?"

I guessed this was Marie. She was probably in her fifties, hair streaked with gray through the natural brown, with a slim waist and a patterned dress trimmed with lace. Modest outfit, but nice. She smiled at me as I looked around.

"Looking for something special for that certain someone?"

On impulse, I asked if she had any white roses.

"Well, we do have some white rosebuds if that would work for you."

"That would be great. I only need one."

She was surprised, but smiled anyway and went into the back of the shop. A minute later she came out with it wrapped in green tissue paper.

"Would you like a box for that?"

I smiled and shook my head. "This is just what I need, nothing fancy."

"Aren't roses always fancy?" I noticed a glimmer in her eye as she said that.

"Well, I guess you're right about that."

As I walked out the door, she said, "You hurry back!"

Instead of my short-cut home, I headed south for a few blocks until I got to Belle Chasse, and turned west to walk by the abandoned house I saw the day before.

I didn't see her anywhere around when I got there. She probably wouldn't talk to strangers anyway, and that would be a good thing. So I stood by the fence for a few minutes looking over the place and wondering what kind of history the house had that had brought it to this. When it was new, I'm sure it was quite grand with the rounded front portico and the two white columns, though now the paint on them was peeling.

After a few minutes, I unlatched the gate and as it swung open it creaked loud enough to wake the neighbors. There was little activity anywhere on the street at the moment, so I walked up to the front door and put the rosebud in front of it. Maybe she would find it, maybe not. Maybe I was just being stupid.

As I turned to leave, I saw a small piece of yellow tape tied around one of the metal side rails. It wasn't clear what it was doing there and, come to think of it, I didn't belong there either, so I hurried away before anyone showed up with questions.

One more look around from the sidewalk didn't turn up anything new, so I went back to the apartment. A good dose of single malt Scotch was next on my agenda, as I sat on the little balcony watching the sunset and wondering about the girl's empty stare.

CHAPTER 3

The next day at work was very busy, mostly with meetings which accomplished, well, nothing. Even so, I was tired of it by five o'clock and more than happy to head out the door. Once again I headed for the short-cut home, and once again got distracted.

As I walked into Marie's, the owner looked up and gave me a smile. "Well, well. Two days in a row. You're one of my best customers!" she said with a chuckle. "What can I get for you? Going to go for two rosebuds today?"

Her charm was infectious and I couldn't help but laugh. "No, I think I'll just stick with one. Don't want to push my luck quite yet." Not entirely accurate, but I wanted to play along. I felt my face getting warm as I said it, embarrassed though not sure why.

"Yes-sirree, sometimes it's better to take things nice and slow. But we do that a lot down here... must be the weather." She disappeared into the back and came out moments later with my one white rosebud, wrapped in tissue. "Will there be anything else?"

"No, this will do it for today. If I keep this up, I'm going to have to ask for a volume discount."

She laughed as she took my money and then I walked out the door.

It was cooler than the day before, more of what you would expect for spring, so the walk over to Belle Chasse was very pleasant and I found the day's tensions draining away as I browsed through the neighborhood, looking at the different home styles, the trees, the gardens. It was a nice part of town here, quite different from the hectic streets of Chicago.

As I slowed down in front of the house, I noticed a neighbor pulling into his driveway. He nodded and pulled his car into the garage behind his house.

From the sidewalk, I couldn't see the rose I'd left the prior day, so I went into the yard and back up on the porch. It was gone, and I felt a brief chill as I wondered if she had found it. I left the new one and then walked back to the sidewalk before anyone got suspicious.

I leaned on the wobbly fence and looked around, hoping to catch a glimpse of her again, but nothing caught my eye until I noticed the neighbor walking up his driveway. He looked over and came down the sidewalk to talk.

"This one needs a lot of work if you're thinking about buying it." He was pleasant enough as he pulled a pipe out of his suit coat and proceeded to fill it. Raising his pipe, he smiled, "They don't let us smoke at work anymore, so I have to sneak one of these whenever I can."

"Well, I suspect this isn't in my price range anyway, but it must have been beautiful in its prime."

"That it was. The owner was a fanatic about roses and covered the entire yard with them. His gardener came here every couple of days to take care of them, and in summer it was quite a sight to see. Flowers everywhere—reds and whites and yellows and oranges. That's why he didn't want any trees. Said they would interfere with the roses. After a while, we all started calling it Rose House.

"He kept the house immaculate too, always had someone here touching up paint or working on some project. It sure was pretty in its day. What brings you to this part of town?"

"Well, originally I was just walking through a lot of the neighborhoods near downtown to see what they were like. I expect I'll be looking to buy something once I get some issues settled. But then this house caught my eye. I noticed the little girl playing in the yard and wondered how someone could live here and leave it like this."

His puzzled look surprised me. "Girl? What girl? This house is empty and has been for years."

"Probably one of the neighbors' kids, then. Saw her standing over by the bench there behind the weeds." I pointed in the general direction.

His face grew more serious and he turned to look where I pointed. "Not a lot of young kids around here, but I think one of the families down the street has some out-of-town visitors. What did she look like?"

"Cute girl, probably around eight or nine, curly blond hair down around her shoulders. I think she wore a white dress, and she had a rose that she held up by her face."

His face turned dark and he scowled at me. "See here, we don't need any of your kind around here. You'd best be gone before I call the police."

I stood there, shocked for a moment by his sudden change of mood, then mumbled, "Sure," and started away.

I didn't bother to turn... but what had just happened? One minute we were having a normal conversation and then he goes off the deep end... for what?

As I turned the corner I did look back. He still stood there glaring at me.

CHAPTER 4

The next morning was rainy and chilly and the forecast called for showers all day, so I opted to drive to work. I went down Belle Chasse on the way into the office but saw nothing unusual. No one walking around today, not that I'd expected it.

Fortunately, things at the office were a lot quieter and more productive than the day before, so I wrapped things up and left a little early. Before I hopped into my car, I made a quick stop at the florist and picked up another rosebud, still bothered by the girl's desolate expression.

The rain had let up some when I stopped in front of Rose House, but I paused a minute, looking around before I got out. No one was outside anywhere on the block, but I had this feeling that I would see the girl again sometime. I left the rose on the porch and again the prior one was gone. I suspected that the neighbor picked them up and threw them out, but who knew?

I looked around briefly and saw nothing out of the ordinary, then headed back to my apartment for a quiet evening.

Thursday morning the streets were still wet, though it was clear again, so I went back to walking. The exercise was apparently doing me some good; I'd lost a couple pounds in the last few weeks.

It was another quiet day in the office and I caught up on the backlog that had magically appeared in my inbox the night before. As I grabbed my coat and walked towards the door, Roger called out to me. "Hey, Lou, are you getting behind on parking tickets already?" I threw him a quizzical glance and saw him motioning to a tall, attractive woman in a drab overcoat standing at the front desk. "Police are looking for you."

The first thing that came to mind was the neighbor from two days ago, but why he would involve the police was beyond me, so I walked over. "How can I help you?"

"Sergeant Sandi Johnson, local police department. You're Lou Navelliere?"

"Yes, what can I do for you?"

"I was wondering if we could talk for a few minutes?" She paused. "It might be better if we went somewhere else, but you're not in trouble and not behind on parking tickets." She grinned as she said that; must have heard Roger.

"I was heading out for the day. Have any suggestions?"

"Well, I'm almost off duty myself, so how about we go over to the Tea Shoppe and I'll buy you a beer?"

That struck me as an odd offer, but I saw no real reason to object, so we went out the door and down the street.

When we walked into the bar, it was moderately crowded and a little noisy, but she steered me to a quiet booth in the back, away from the main room. She didn't say anything until we'd ordered our beers, and then picked a couple of nuts out of the bowl on the table and popped them into her mouth.

Was she deliberately stalling? I had no reason to worry that I could think of, so I sat there watching.

Our waitress showed up with our order and then left.

"Sorry, I didn't get around to lunch today, so I'm pretty hungry. Like I said, you're not in any trouble, but I just want to understand something. A couple of days ago you were talking to a gentleman over on Belle Chasse, is that correct?"

"Sure. I had noticed the empty house next to his and was looking at it when he came over. We talked for a few minutes but then he seemed to get very upset and told me I should get out of there. I wasn't sure what prompted that, it caught me completely by surprise. So I just left. I looked back from the end of the block and he was still staring at me. Why would he call the police about it?"

"For openers, the man you talked to is Reeve Marchant, one of the city commissioners. He called the office the next morning and I picked up the call. Said I'd check it out for him."

"Has he filed a complaint of some kind against me?"

"No, nothing like that. It was something you said that got him concerned. We like to keep our neighborhoods safe. I'm sure you understand that."

"Well, of course, but I didn't do anything wrong, and it is a public street."

She continued, "Why don't you just tell me why you were there that day? And yesterday for that matter."

"How did you know I was there yesterday. Am I being followed? For that matter, how did you even find me?"

"Look, don't get upset. I just need some answers, so why don't you tell me why you were there that day?"

I had the distinct feeling this wasn't going well, but I didn't see that I had much choice. I took a long swallow of beer while I studied her face for a moment and tried to figure out how to answer.

"Am I being charged with a crime?"

She shook her head. "No, you are not in trouble. You're not being charged with anything. I just want to know what you were doing there."

"Do I have to answer your questions?"

"No, you're free to leave if you want." She paused with an exasperated expression. "But there are some things you are probably not aware of. If you just give me some answers, I'll explain what this is about and I think we can be done with it."

In reality, she was reasonably nice, but she sure wasn't answering any of my questions. I paused again, frustrated, but then there was nothing for me to hide.

"Okay, I looked at the house. I'm new in town and I walk to work when the weather is good, to get some exercise and maybe lose a few pounds. I got tired of taking the short way and started taking different routes. A week or so ago I went down Belle Chasse and noticed this big, empty house in disrepair sitting in the middle of a block of very well-kept homes. It intrigued me.

"I've always liked older houses with their high ceilings and fancy trim, though it's not something in my budget. I appreciate them, though, and I can look. That's all I was doing there. The neighbor happened to come home when I was standing on the sidewalk looking at it and he struck up a conversation."

She looked at me skeptically for a minute without saying anything, then had another sip of beer. "So, what's with the rose?"

I had been waiting for that to come up. A middle-aged man leaving roses for a very young girl was probably cause for suspicion. "Okay, the first time I saw the house I noticed a young girl behind some of the bushes. I only saw her for a moment, but she was crying and had a kind of haunted look in her eyes."

"Interesting choice of words. Go on."

"Look, I think I see where you're going with this, but it meant nothing. She just seemed so miserable and upset I thought leaving a rose would make her happy. It's nothing. I'm not a pervert, if that is what you are thinking."

She looked up. "Yeah, I know. I checked your background."

I stopped short and stared at her.

"Originally from New Orleans. Down here from the Chicago area for a job transfer. No known violations except for speeding tickets and, come to think of it, you have an outstanding parking ticket up there. You should probably take care of that. Other than that, you're pretty much straight and narrow."

I had no idea how to respond and just stared. What was going on?

"Tell me more about the girl."

"I didn't get a good look at her, really. She seemed about eight years old, and like I said, she was crying. She had curly hair...lots of curls. Then I got distracted and when I turned back around she was gone."

She looked at me sideways. "Anything else?"

"Oh, yeah. She held a rose up next to her face. That kind of struck me as odd."

"Would you recognize her if you saw her again?"

"Pretty sure I would. It was mostly the look in her eyes that caught my attention."

She reached into her coat pocket and pulled out a dog-eared photograph which she proceeded to look at. "I want you to take a look at this and tell me if you recognize anyone here."

The photo was worn from handling, but still clear. A family group stood in front of the house: husband, wife, two boys, the girl, and then another younger girl in the mother's arms. Her face jumped right out at me and I knew instantly it was the same girl, though maybe a little younger.

"That's her to the right of the woman. This is a family photo, I assume?"

The sergeant watched my face very closely. "Are you positive this is the same girl?"

"Yeah, sure. The photo looks like she might have been a year or two younger, but it is definitely her."

"This is the girl you saw in the yard, right?"

I was not sure at all where this was going. With the picture, the officer seemed very serious. "Yes, taken maybe a year ago or so, but definitely her. The hair is done up the same way." Then I noticed something else. "And she even has a rose in her hand."

She paused for a moment. "Sara."

I was confused for a moment, then realized what she meant. "That's her name?"

She smiled sadly. "Yes." Then, after a pause, "She would have turned fifteen last month."

My jaw dropped and I stared, trying to piece this together. It took me a few moments before I asked, "Is this some kind of a joke?"

"Funny, I was thinking of asking you the same thing."

My mind spun. This was too weird.

"So, Johnson, you're telling me that she's a ghost?"

"Well, actually, I think *you're* telling *me* that, and honestly, I don't like it." She frowned across the table while the waitress brought us another round of beers, then continued, "Look, there is no girl.

She's been dead for seven years now. It'll be easier if you leave the house alone and forget it."

I shook my head. "Then how did I identify her?"

Johnson obviously didn't want to have this conversation. "Look, just drop it and leave the place alone and we'll all be happy."

I remembered the girl's eyes, and the rose. It wouldn't be that simple for me. God, she even showed up in my dreams. "Fine, easy for you. Look, I don't see ghosts, they don't exist. But I can look up the history of the house to find out whatever there is to know. It's not something I'm just going to drop."

She pressed her lips together and frowned at me for a long time. "Okay, let me explain the situation, then maybe you'll let this rest. Harper and Stella Dylan lived in Rose House for years, long before I got here. They had four children: twin boys Max and Owen, Sara, who you identified, and then another daughter, Libby, who was under two.

"By all accounts from neighbors and people that knew them, they were a normal family with a few quirks. Planting the entire yard in roses was one of them, but it's hardly a crime. But one night a neighbor heard a noise that he thought was a gunshot—only one, no other noises. He went over and knocked on the door to check on them, but no one answered. Since he wasn't really sure what he heard, he just went home and forgot about it. A couple of days later he rang the doorbell again and got the same result. At that point, he got worried and called the police."

As Johnson took a long sip of beer, I noticed that her hands were shaking. "I had just moved into town and joined the department and my boss told me to go over and check it out. When I got there, the gardener was banging on the back door. He said he was supposed to get paid that day and no one was home. He was pretty upset about it, said he needed the money to pay his rent.

"The doors were all locked, but I got lucky. I found an unlocked window off the back porch and climbed in that way. The minute I got inside I knew something was very wrong, just from the smell. Metallic, like drying blood. I called for backup immediately and went to unlock the front door, but on the way I passed the dining room.

"Stella was lying on the floor in a pool of blood from a head wound. There was blood everywhere, and I could tell she was dead. When backup got there, we went through the whole house.

"Sara was upstairs in her bedroom and she looked unconscious, but when I checked for a pulse, she was totally cold. Same thing with the baby Libby. Harper, the father, slumped in a chair behind his desk in the study. He had a massive hole through the back of his head and a handgun was lying on the floor next to him.

"At first glance, it looked like Harper killed the others and then himself, but that left a problem: where were the twin boys?"

She took another drink, trying to stay calm, but it seemed like she was losing the battle.

"All of this is a matter of public record, so I'm not letting out anything you shouldn't know. I got assigned to investigate the case and worked on it for the next year, in between other jobs.

"The twins were never found. Sara and Libby had been suffocated with something, probably a pillow from their bed. Stella wasn't so lucky. It looked like she had been trying to get away when she was attacked. Her skull was cracked and it appeared she had been hit repeatedly, possibly even after she was unconscious.

"Harper's death was ruled a suicide and we believe he also killed his wife and daughters. We never came up with a reason why. Technically the case is still open, but we have nowhere to go with it. Before we were finished, we went through the entire house. We found a relatively large amount of cash and a little jewelry, but they lived in the wealthiest neighborhood in town, so that was no surprise.

"Which brings us back to Reeve and his comments to you. After the story hit the papers, people showed up out of nowhere, saying that they had a psychic connection to the family or the house, or that they talked to the ghosts. It really got out of hand for a while, for over two years. When Reeve called, he mentioned to me that he was afraid it was going to start all over again."

I looked at her, at a loss for words. And then I remembered Sara's face in the garden. "When I saw her behind the bench, Sara was crying. Any ideas about that?"

Johnson shook her head. "The parents were apparently pretty strict and kept their kids out of sight, but the neighbors all said the kids were normal, if a little quiet. They were pretty good students, too—not exceptional but they got A's and B's most of the time. Not the picture of kids that are under stress. So no, no idea what the tears are about. So what is your part in this, Lou? Going to solve the mystery for us?" She grimaced, skeptical.

I shook my head, not sure where to start. "Look, I knew nothing about any of this. I just saw her in the overgrown garden and for some reason it stuck with me. I'm not trying to drag this up again; that's the last thing I want. I'm not even sure what on earth to think about it all."

Johnson watched me for a few minutes, saying nothing. "You don't seem at all like the others who came around after the murders. They all had lots of ideas and wanted to talk to the papers. Looked like it was mostly for publicity. You don't strike me as the type."

My thoughts kept bouncing back to the image of Sara. "Is there something significant about the rose?"

She looked up, curious. "Yeah, I didn't mention that. Seems that the girl loved roses and always carried one around with her wherever she went."

"Okay, one more question...how come the house is just sitting there falling apart? Don't the heirs want it sold for the money?"

Johnson shook her head again. "Well, they probably would if there were some. That's another dead end. When we investigated, we looked everywhere but found no living relatives. Actually, at one point we thought there might have been someone else in the family involved in the deaths, but there was no one we could find. So the house just sits there. The city tried to sell it for back taxes, but no one even showed up to make an offer. Can't say I blame them with a history like that."

"Look, Johnson," I said, "the last thing I want is to make this into a problem for you. I walked into this blind and had no idea what the history was. I'm not sure what to do at this point."

"Maybe you should just leave it alone. Forget about it… the house, the girl, the whole story."

I paused a long time, thinking about Sara, her tears, her eyes. "I don't know if I can."

Johnson shook her head again. "I was afraid you'd say that." She paused for a few moments. "Look, it's getting late. Did you drive into work today?"

It struck me as another odd question. "No, I walked again, like I usually do."

"Then let me give you a ride home. It's right on my way anyway."

I thought about it for a minute, then declined.

Her lips pulled tight and her eyes narrowed, then she shook her head slightly. "You're going by Rose House, aren't you?"

Well, that was probably an easy guess for her. "Yes, I am."

She sighed. "Fine, I'll take you by there first. You get out and look around, and if Reeve comes out at least there won't be a scene; I need to talk to him anyway."

I saw no reason not to have her along, and I couldn't stop her anyway, so I agreed and we went back towards the office where her car was parked. The flower shop was closed for the night, which was no surprise, but as we walked by the front door I noticed a package lying on the ground in the alcove. When I picked it up, I saw a note on it. "Louis, this one is on the house. Marie." Inside was a white rosebud.

Johnson read it over my shoulder, then shook her head again. "Now I know you're in this way too deep. It's a conspiracy!"

When we got to Rose House, we both got out of the car and crossed over to the fence. She stayed there while I went to put the rose on the porch. The prior one was gone, as usual.

"Did Reeve say anything about picking up the roses I put on the porch?" I asked.

"No, he did say he went up to look a few times but never found anything there; thought it was a little strange, but he wasn't sure what you were doing. Why do you ask?"

"They're always gone the next day."

She closed her eyes for a moment. "Somehow I wish I hadn't heard that."

CHAPTER 5

A couple of days later I took the afternoon off work. I'd just had a less than pleasant conversation with my wife Clara in Chicago about the divorce, and was still upset. It was an uncontested divorce and we normally got along fairly well, even now, but every once in a while something came up that would set me off, usually in the area of who got to keep what. All the furniture stayed there with her, so when things finally settled I would need to get my stuff and bring it down here, probably to put it in storage somewhere until I bought a place.

We'd always gotten along very well until we hit on some basic issues that we should have discussed before we got married, like having kids. That one blew up in our faces. Still, I missed Clara a lot, but what can you do? She was totally opposed to having children and I had always assumed they were part of the package. We were still young enough, but I couldn't change her mind and I didn't really want to because then she wouldn't be happy.

I understood her decision and respected it, but it wasn't my decision.

So, after a heated discussion about why I should keep some heirlooms from my family rather than let her have them, I wanted to get out of the office and calm down.

I left the office and went over to Belle Chasse, as usual, after a brief stop at Marie's. Since the morning had been rainy, I'd driven into work, but I figured that now, in the middle of the afternoon, no one would be around to take notice of a car parked out on the street.

The rain let up some when I got out and I took my time looking around. Nothing was different at all, so I went up to the porch to drop off the rose. I set it right in front of the door and then turned around. The small piece of yellow tape still fluttered in the breeze on the side railing, but now I noticed the word 'police' on what remained.

I thought I heard a noise over toward the side of the house and turned to look, but saw nothing. As I started to turn back, I saw something white out of the corner of my eye. White dress, blond curls, white rose. I stood there staring at her, while she looked back at me.

I barely whispered it. "Hello, Sara."

She tilted her head a little, so I thought maybe she'd heard me, but I wasn't sure. She just watched.

What do you say to a ghost? Tell her she's pretty? That sure seemed dumb. Try to have a conversation? If she actually said something, I would have bolted. As it was, I felt the sweat running down my back. The temperature hovered in the low 60s.

"Is there something I can do for you?"

No response.

Flustered, scared, and confused, I started to turn away, then looked at her again. "I'll be back." Then I started walking towards my car. I glanced over my shoulder again but she was gone.

As I looked around, I saw Johnson leaning against my car, watching me.

"Are you following me?"

"No, just passing through the neighborhood and saw you here. You're early today. Trying to throw me off?"

I shook my head. "Surely you have something better to do than this? Go catch some robbers or give out some speeding tickets."

That got a slight grin, but then she turned serious again. "Looked like you were talking to someone."

I wasn't sure how much I wanted to say, but then she already knew why I was here. "She was there again. Second time I've seen her. Looked about the same as last time, but I think I saw a reaction when

I said her name. I'm surprised you didn't barge up the walk to see if you could see anything."

Half of her mouth went up, the other half down, and she leaned back against my car. "You know, my husband's grandmother does this stuff about seeing ghosts and talking with the dead. I always thought she was loony, but she's in her nineties and she's family, so what do you do? If she heard that I did something like that she would probably make a voodoo doll of me and start sticking pins in it.

"By the way, I talked to Reeve and told him you were harmless and weren't going to make a spectacle of yourself. Don't prove me wrong."

"Wouldn't think of it. Anything else you need from me?"

"Nah, have a good evening."

As I started to drive away, a thought occurred to me and I turned right and headed back downtown to the library.

The librarian on duty was very helpful and pointed me to the periodicals section. When I asked about older newspapers, she showed me the microfiche reels. "Sorry, but we aren't finished converting to online yet. Is there something I can help you find?"

When I mentioned an old crime from seven or eight years ago, her eyebrows went up. "Rose House?"

"Yes, please. Get a lot of inquiries for that?"

"We used to, but it dropped off after the first year or so. This is the first time anyone mentioned it in a couple of years, at least. Let me see what I can find for you."

Three hours later I was tired, hungry, and disappointed. The newspaper accounts had a few more details than I'd gotten from Johnson, but much of it was speculation. Basically, everything checked out exactly the way I first heard it. And then, not for the first time, I wondered exactly where I was going with this.

CHAPTER 6

The following day I took a long lunch and went down to City Hall to do some more research. I was just walking out of the office when I heard someone call my name. Johnson, of course.

"Now I *know* you're following me."

She grinned. "Nope. Small town, you know. I picked up some paperwork for another case. I do have some other things to work on. You know, robbers and speeding tickets." She glanced at the wall behind me. "What brings you down to the Assessor's office? Trouble with taxes already? On your apartment?"

I looked a little sheepish and just said, "I was just checking out a few things, nothing important."

She looked closely at me. "Does this have anything to do with Rose House?"

While I didn't want to tell her what I was doing, I also didn't want to lie. "Yeah, just checking up on some facts."

She got a curious look on her face. "At the Assessor's office." Then, she backed off a step with a shocked look. "Wait, you're not thinking of buying it, are you?" She paused while I said nothing. "God, Lou, are you crazy? Come with me, we need to have a talk before you do something really stupid."

"Look, I've got to get back to work. We can talk some other time."

She knew I was trying to get out of this. "Fine, after work tonight at the Tea Shoppe. I'll be in the side room waiting for you."

I shrugged. "Okay, sure."

***

When I got there later, she was sitting in the same spot. "Do you have this booth reserved or something?"

Ignoring me, she said, "Please tell me you are *not* thinking about buying Rose House."

"You know, Johnson, this is not really any of your business."

"First of all, call me Sandi. This is not official, and yes, you are right, it is none of my business and I can't stop you from doing that if you want." She paused for a fraction of a second. "Even if it is incredibly stupid."

"And why would it be stupid? It's a lovely old house that needs some work and I might be able to pick it up for back taxes since no one else is interested."

"There are several reasons no one else is interested. First of all, it's been sitting there for seven years with minimal maintenance, so you have no idea what kind of damage has been done. Second, you can't get in to look around or have it inspected if you want to buy it since it's a foreclosure, so you're going in blind. Third, it's a crime scene! I remember the blood all over the carpet and it's been there for seven years. Oh, did I mention it's a crime scene? Four people *died* in that house and it was pretty gruesome. I would know, I spent a lot of time in there. And two more disappeared. Oh, yeah, and it apparently has a ghost.

"Why don't you just go buy a newer place a mile or so south of town? There are some nice developments down there for decent prices. Hell, I'll even take you myself if you want. We can go on Saturday, I'm off then for a change."

I saw she was getting worked up about this, but it didn't have the effect she wanted. "Look, I can be stubborn. The more you try to talk me out of this, the more I think it is a good idea."

She stared at me for a moment. "Sure, and a bunch of people came up with another great idea: buy tickets on the Titanic."

"Besides that, it seems like I'm the only one who sees this ghost. She has shown no indications that she means any harm. It almost seems like she wants me to help her, though I have no idea why or what for."

Sandi covered her eyes for a moment with her hand before trying another tack. "You know, there are some good psychiatrists who would be more than happy to talk to you at length about this. I bet I can talk a couple of them into giving you a complimentary session to get you started, no strings attached."

"Do I detect a hint of sarcasm here?"

"God, I hope so. Anyway, I thought you were in the middle of a divorce. Don't you have to wrap that up first?"

"Is there anything about me you *don't* know?"

"Waist size?"

"Very funny. I probably should wait until the divorce gets settled rather than confuse the issue. I might be able to swing it if I wanted to and the back taxes aren't too bad."

"You'll have a hard time getting a loan on Rose House. Too many people here remember the stories and want nothing to do with it."

"If we're just talking back taxes, or something close, I won't need a loan."

Sandi was hard to persuade. "But what about the thousands of dollars you'll need to clean it up and make it livable, assuming that is even possible?"

"Gotta do something with all this money I make working nine to five. Can't think of a better project, really."

She stared at me. "Lou, I worry about you... a lot."

CHAPTER 7

The phone woke me up. The clock said 11:30, so I'd only been asleep for a little while, but it seemed like forever. I grabbed my phone and recognized the number: Matt Rhoades was a friend and next-door neighbor from Chicago. Clara and I had hung out with him and his wife Marta. "Matt, how are you?" I mumbled.

"Hey, Lou, sounds like I woke you up."

"I just climbed into bed. What's up?"

"I have some bad news, Lou. Clara was in an accident earlier this evening. She's over at Suburban General right now. I thought I'd better give you a call and let you know."

I snapped totally awake. "What happened? How bad is it?"

"Well, it's not good, I can tell you that, but the doctors aren't sure yet. They're still running tests, but she hasn't regained consciousness since she got there. She was broadsided by a guy in an SUV who tried to pass her when she was turning left into your driveway. I guess he didn't see her turn signal. The police aren't saying anything more than that at the moment, but I have to wonder if he had been drinking."

"What kind of injuries?"

"Head trauma, some broken ribs. Not sure what else, but I figured you should know as soon as possible."

"Yeah, thanks. I don't think I can catch a flight up tonight, but I'll get one in the morning."

"That should be good. Even if she comes around tonight, she's going to need a lot of rest anyway. I'm sure she'll be glad to see you. And let me know when your flight is coming in, I'll pick you up at the airport."

"Yeah, Okay, thanks. Hey, Matt, can you check on Furb for me, just to make sure he's okay?"

"Marta already took care of that. We might bring him over to our house tomorrow so he has someone to play with."

"Yeah, great, I should have known you would have things under control. Thanks again."

"Sure, talk to you tomorrow."

I climbed out of bed, started a pot of coffee, and turned on the computer.

***

After getting the reservations made, I only got about three hours of sleep before the alarm went off. The flight wasn't for several hours, but it would be an hour drive to the airport, so I didn't have a lot of time.

I called into the office as soon as it opened and explained the situation to my boss. He was good about it, said to take whatever time I needed. Since I was still the new guy on the block, he was used to covering things.

I grabbed my travel bag and was about to go to my car when I had another thought. I looked around through my paperwork and found Johnson's business card with her cell number, so I gave her a call.

"Hey, Sandi, it's Lou. Do you have a minute?"

"Sure, what's up? I'm just about a block away from your place anyway. Want to get some donuts?"

I briefly explained what had happened and told her I was catching a flight out in a little while. Not sure when I would be back.

"You planning to leave your car at the airport? That could get pricey depending on how long you're gone. I'll give you a ride if you like."

"No, I'll be good. Thanks for the offer. But there is one thing you could do for me while I'm gone. Can you take a rose over there every day, please?"

She paused for a moment, probably thinking I was crazy, then said. "Sorry, Lou. No way. I could lose my job over that."

"Okay, never mind."

"And Lou, sorry to hear about your wife. Hope it works out okay."

I was surprised, but maybe I shouldn't have been. "Thanks, Sandi."

CHAPTER 8

Matt was tied up in a meeting when my flight arrived, so his wife Marta and their three-year-old son MJ picked me up at the airport. Marta was in her mid-thirties, slim and trim and normally full of energy, but today she was subdued as she gave me a hug.

I picked up MJ and gave him a big hug too. "Hey there, big guy. You've grown about three feet since I saw you last!"

He just giggled.

Marta was very quiet until we got into the car. "I stopped by the hospital this morning but saw no change. Clara is still in a coma. God, Lou, I'm sorry. I know it's a big mess with the divorce and all, but even so... you two were so close."

"Yeah, I know. It's odd. I still love her. I wish this divorce wasn't happening, but if we had kids she would have resented me for pushing her, and if we didn't, then I'd feel like I was missing out on something important. Even with all that, I would have stayed, but then she decided it was best for me if we split."

"I know. I remember the arguments you two got into on occasion. It's a shame how it turned out."

"Marta, is there any more information on how the accident happened? It seemed a little odd to me. Clara was always such a careful driver."

"Apparently she had worked later than usual and was coming home around 7:30. When she slowed to turn left into your driveway this guy swung around her to pass and broadsided the driver's side. Turns out he was drinking and well over the legal limit at the time. He also wound up in the hospital but he's out now. And he has several prior DUIs on his record. Personally, I hope they lock him up forever."

"What about Clara? Matt didn't really tell me how badly she was hurt."

Marta glanced over before answering, like she wasn't sure I was ready for this. "Well, we know more now than last night. Three broken ribs, broken arm. But the fractured skull is the worst part of it. The doctors seemed a little surprised she was alive when she got there." She started crying, wiping the tears away as she drove. "God, Lou, I don't know what to say. We just want her back. She was always so much fun to be with, like the sister I wish I had."

She turned into their driveway as I looked over at our house next door with totally mixed emotions. "Thanks for taking care of Furball."

She shut off the car and reached over to give me a hug. "We miss you both so much."

"Yeah, I miss you guys too."

I helped her get MJ out of the car, then grabbed my bag and headed next door.

"Lou, if it's easier for you, you can stay in our guest bedroom."

I thought about it briefly. "Thanks, but I think it will be okay. The cat needs someone around anyway."

She smiled warmly. "I'm making a big pot of stew if you want to come over later. You know you're always welcome. And you can use the car whenever you want, just knock on the door." She paused, "But I guess you know that by now."

I nodded and carried my bag across the lawn. I had no sooner walked in the front door before Furb showed up, sixteen pounds of Maine Coon cat, and trotted quickly over to say hello, rubbing against my legs, and then letting me pick him up and scratch behind his ears like I used to. It was great to see him again and I carried him around with me, talking to him and petting him until he'd had enough, then I took my bag into the bedroom.

Like always, the bed was neatly made and everything was picked up around the house. The only thing sitting out was the coffee cup from breakfast. Clara always left it out so she could have another cup when she came home from work.

Being back here in the house suddenly brought back so many memories. I sat down on the couch, wiping the tears off my face, remembering the way things used to be and all of the fun, and arguments, we'd had. Now I wished I had done more to try to make it work, to change her mind about the divorce. Furb came by and rubbed against my legs, then jumped up on the couch and curled up next to me, watching.

We'd met at my cousin's wedding about ten years ago. I had been working for a couple of years and she was graduating from college and looking for a job. I asked her to dance and we hit it off right away. Clara was always easy to talk to, open, but she also spoke her mind. That was a nice change from the other women I had dated; I'd always had to guess what they wanted, but not with Clara. I remember her telling me she wanted a job in downtown Chicago, a small house in the suburbs and a cat named Furball. It was so specific that I leaned away from her in the middle of the dance and looked into her eyes, amazed. I was hooked right then.

We also had a lot in common with the books we read, the movies we liked—my favorite was Blade Runner, but she was more of a Trekkie. Still, it was only a couple of months later that we moved in together, and then about a year later I proposed, though she later admitted she wished I had done that sooner.

I remembered all of the Saturday mornings I would get up early and go out to get her a caramel latte, her Saturday extravagance. She loved waking up to that smell.

I wiped my tears one last time and checked to make sure Furb had water and food, rubbed behind his ears again and told him I would be back later, then called a cab for the trip to the hospital.

CHAPTER 9

The nurse in intensive care asked apologetically for some ID. "Sorry. Technically we are only supposed to let family in, though I know her neighbors have been coming to see her."

I showed her my driver's license. "I'm the only family she has left, so I'm glad they're watching out for her."

Handing me back my license, she nodded and showed me to Clara's room.

I'm not sure what I'd expected, even after Marta's description, but I was shocked when I walked in the door. Clara's entire head was bandaged except for her face. Her left arm was in a cast, lying on top of the covers. There were oxygen tubes, feeding tubes, and wires everywhere.

She appeared to be sleeping, and I wished that were the case. Her face looked a little thinner than when I'd last seen her a few months ago, but I wasn't sure if that was from the accident or whether she had lost weight lately. She certainly didn't need to lose any more weight; she had always been thin.

I put my hand on hers but got no reaction. She felt chilly, but the room was cold. So I pulled up a chair and sat, watching her face for any sign of movement. A few minutes later I noticed tears running down my cheeks again.

I wanted to talk to her, but I wasn't at all sure where to start. Though the divorce was amicable, it still hurt after nine years of marriage, and now to see her like this...

"Clara, it's Lou. I've missed you so much. When I heard about what happened I caught the first flight up here to see you." Words failed me, and I just sat there holding her hand.

About ten minutes later, a doctor came into the room. He was tall, thin, probably in his late fifties with graying hair. Wiping the tears from my face, I introduced myself as he held out his hand.

"I'm Doctor Armstrong. You're her husband?"

"Yes, living in Louisiana now while the divorce is going on, so it took me a bit to get up here."

He looked at my red eyes. "I'm sorry you have to see her like this. It's difficult enough going through something like that."

"What can you tell me about her condition?"

He paused for a moment then said, "Let's go for a walk. Looks like we could both use some coffee."

We got the coffee and found a quiet corner of the cafeteria to sit. It was fairly empty with the lunch crowd finally clearing out.

"Her condition is very serious, as you probably guessed. The arm and the ribs are broken, but that will heal in time. There don't appear to be any internal injuries or bleeding. The fractured skull is much more serious. She has been in a coma since she got here." He looked steadily at me. "We have no way to know when she will come out of it," he paused, "or even *if* she will come out of it. She could come around tomorrow or it could be months. We just can't tell."

"Is there anything I can do for her other than just be here? Anything you need to know?"

He shook his head slowly. "That is about the best you can do for now. Talking to her might help. Sometimes they can hear you even if they can't respond."

He looked around the room, making sure no one could hear us. "Can I ask you some personal questions?"

I was surprised. "Sure, I'll do anything to help her."

"What was the reason for the divorce? Was there another person involved?"

I looked at him quizzically. "No, it was nothing like that. Neither of us was having an affair, we just kept getting into arguments about having children and neither of us wanted to change our mind."

He tilted his head slightly. "She wanted them and you didn't?"

"No, it was the other way around. She just didn't feel like she was up to being a mother. Maybe the idea intimidated her, she never told me why. Why are you asking this?"

"One more question. When was the last time you were intimate?"

"Why do you need to know that?"

"Please, humor me for a moment."

"It was right before I left town several months ago. Even though we argued and filed for divorce, we still got along. We stilled loved each other."

"Sorry to have to pry into this, but I needed to know. As we were running our usual battery of tests, we found out that she is pregnant, close to three months along."

I sat there staring at him for a long time, my eyes wide. "We've talked since then on occasion, but she never said a word about it. I can't imagine what she was going through; she must have known. Why didn't she tell me?"

"As you can imagine, this complicates her treatment immensely. We have to be very careful what we give her, but our first priority is to save her life. We're trying to be as conservative as possible to protect the child." He paused for a moment. "She never said anything to you, or gave you any hints?"

"No, nothing. This changes everything."

"Again, pardon me for asking this, but can we get a sample of your DNA?"

"Yes, of course."

We stood to go and I walked blindly out of the cafeteria, shocked. I wondered what she had been thinking.

CHAPTER 10

The next few days went very slowly and started to run together. I spent each day and most of the evenings at the hospital, hoping for Clara to come around, but there was nothing so far. The doctors were still saying the same things: you can't tell with something like this; it could be days or months.

In the meantime, I tried to talk to her about some of the good times we had, like the time we went for a day hike in the White Mountains during a trip through New England. She was never much for the outdoors until we took that trip. Looking out over New Hampshire and Maine had brought a new perspective that really opened her eyes. We hiked a lot more after that, much of it at her suggestion.

I talked to her about the time we'd spent with the M&M's, as we called Marta and Matt, and then MJ too. We spent a lot of evenings and weekends with them, going out to dinner, watching movies, and just sitting around talking, and always got along very well. Good times... that was what I tried to focus on.

Then each evening I'd go home. I still thought of it that way, even with my apartment in Louisiana. Apartments just don't feel the same. Usually, I'd spend an hour or two with the neighbors, since Marta insisted that I shouldn't eat hospital cafeteria food all the time. It was nice catching up on some of the things that had changed with them since I'd left. Matt had changed jobs and in the process got a nice promotion, so he was pretty happy about that. Marta had started yoga classes to get herself in shape, though she had been in much better shape before than I ever had been.

At one point in the evening we were talking and I idly asked if Clara had started seeing anyone after I'd left.

After a brief look at each other, they both laughed. "Yes, she's been practically married to her job. Why would you even ask?"

"Oh, nothing, just curious."

Marta got a sad expression on her face. "Lou, she missed you terribly. She'd come over once in a while to just talk. A couple of times we were up until two in the morning remembering the things we did together. Even back when MJ came along it didn't change anything; you two were always there for us. She wasn't even thinking about dating. Are you?"

I told them no, since I hadn't considered it at this point, and then I idly thought about telling her about this eight-year-old I was interested in, but it would have been too weird and they would have thought I was losing it. It felt very odd not being able to talk to my close friends about Sara, but that almost seemed like another world.

Then, shortly after a late dinner, I would walk back home and try to sleep, with a warm cat curled up by my toes.

Thursday morning I got up a little later than usual and called my boss to keep him up to date on the situation. He was still very supportive, but he also caught me by surprise.

"Lou, look, I know these things take a long time, so don't take this the wrong way. I talked to Chris in Chicago the other day, and it might be possible to get you transferred back up to your old job until this gets settled. Now, I really like having you down here. I'm already starting to see some positive changes around the office since you came. Heck, you've even got Roger bringing in business again. But I wanted to mention it in case it's something you feel the need to do."

"I don't know, Ed. Part of the reason for going to Louisiana was the divorce, and part was because it feels like home to me after growing up down there. Honestly, I don't know what the best choice is for me right now, but I know I need to be here for Clara. Even once she comes out of this, it's going to be hard going for her and I want to help. Let me think about that for a while. Thanks for the offer."

"Remember, I'll keep this job open for you, that is not a problem. Just figure out what works out best for you and your wife. I know it has to be rough going through this."

I hung up and grabbed another cup of coffee before I headed over to the hospital.

When I got out of the elevator on the third floor, I saw Dr. Armstrong in the hallway and he motioned me over. "How is Clara doing this morning?"

"No change, really. I keep hoping for her to come around. Do you have a couple of minutes to talk?"

"Sure. Is this about the tests?"

He nodded. "There's an empty room down the hall. Let's go in there and talk."

We sat down in the guest chairs before he started.

"The DNA tests came back. As I suspected, the baby is definitely yours. It's a girl. Now we have another reason to hope Clara comes around soon."

A million different thoughts ran through my mind simultaneously. This was exactly what Clara hadn't wanted, so how had this happened? She wouldn't have done it intentionally; she was never like that and was always up front with what she wanted. That was one of the things I admired most about her. But I had so many questions.

"Is there anything we need to do differently to make sure the baby is okay?"

"We're already doing it. The ultrasound shows she is developing normally, but with Clara in a coma we have no control over this."

Just then his buzzer went off. He looked down at the screen, then looked over at me. "Sorry, but I have to run. Could you go to the waiting room while I look in on Clara?"

Something seemed wrong, but I wasn't sure. I felt a tightness in my stomach. "Sure, I'll do that."

I'd been in the waiting room about half hour when Dr. Armstrong came in. He looked strained and disheveled and very serious. He put his hand on my shoulder. "Lou, I'm sorry. That beep that I got earlier was about Clara. It started with an irregular heart rhythm, but then she shut down all at once. There was very little warning and it happened very fast. I'm sorry, we lost her. We tried everything, but we couldn't save either of them."

I sat there, stunned. "There's nothing you can do?"

"I'm sorry. We tried everything we could."

My world was slipping very much out of control. It had been a little over a week ago that I had been getting used to a new town, a new job, and maybe thinking about buying a house. And in the blink of an eye, I'd lost my wife and the daughter I hadn't even known I had. So fast. I covered my face with my hands and cried.

It took a while before I regained my composure, and Dr. Armstrong waited patiently, giving me time to come to terms with this.

"Can I see her?"

"Of course, but give us a few more minutes. You can wait in here if you like. I'll send someone when we're ready."

I nodded, saying nothing. I just wished I had found something to do differently that would have prevented this. Maybe if we had tried a little harder to make it work. Maybe if I wasn't so stubborn. I don't know… there was no way to know.

The same nurse walked back in. "Mr. Navelliere, I'm so sorry about your wife."

I nodded and got up as she led me to Clara's room. She held the door for me as I walked in, and said, "Take as much time as you need."

Clara looked so peaceful like she always had when she was sleeping. I took her hand in mine; it was still warm. And then I saw it.

Lying on her stomach was a white rosebud.

CHAPTER 11

The next few weeks were a whirlwind. Funeral arrangements needed to be made, which Marta helped with, driving me around and, more importantly, providing moral support. I called Ed in Louisiana and told him I would be back to work in about a week or so. I made arrangements to ship the furniture to Louisiana, figuring it could go into storage until I figured out where I wanted it.

I spent a long time on the phone contacting Clara's friends, including some old college girlfriends she'd met with once a year or so. Some of them who lived in the area had heard about the accident, and one or two people had called the house earlier to check up on how she was doing. They all were upset and promised to be there for the funeral.

The first few evenings I spent with Matt and Marta, talking, reminiscing about places we had gone—the museums, the art shows. But then I started staying in the house by myself, thinking about our time together and how good it had been. I walked into the kitchen one morning and noticed that her coffee cup was still on the counter. I looked at it for a long time before deciding to leave it there.

The day of the funeral was cold and rainy, but Clara used to love rainy weather, so it was peculiarly appropriate. Lots of old friends and people from Clara's job showed up, some of whom I hadn't met before. A luncheon followed the burial, with probably sixty people, and I talked to all of them. Everyone had good things to say about her and I knew she'd be sorely missed. She'd touched people, in one way or another, and it showed. Her three college girlfriends showed up together and each gave me a hug, more for Clara than anything else. The look in their eyes made me wonder if they were thinking "this could have been me."

Matt and Marta, with MJ in tow, walked around, introducing themselves to people they had never met and talking to them. As I watched the pair of them, I realized again how much we would all miss Clara.

And then it all ended and I wound up at Matt and Marta's house—tired, despondent and at a loss for what to do next. When I briefly stopped at home before coming over, not even Furb could cheer me up. He, too, was quieter than usual and I think he knew she was gone for good.

Matt and I were drinking Scotch. I had given him a bottle of single malt about a year ago, but he'd never opened it until now.

We sat there quietly, both lost in our own thoughts when Marta came in after putting MJ down for a nap. He normally hated them, but the day had been exhausting for all of us and he didn't fight it this time.

Marta poured herself some Scotch and sat down next to Matt, watching me. "I'm not sure what we're going to do without her, Lou. She was so much a part of our life for so long." She paused. "But how are you handling it?"

I looked over, avoiding her eyes. "As well as can be expected. I never expected anything like this. I guess we never do, huh?"

Marta waited before responding. "No, we don't. I don't think we can." She paused again for a bit. "Lou, we've known each other for a long time." Another pause. "Is there something you're not telling us?"

I tried to cover my mixed emotions about what to say, but Marta knew me well enough to know a piece was missing. My conversations with Dr. Armstrong were locked up in my head, playing in loops, but I hadn't said anything. I took a large swallow of Scotch. "One other thing came out while she was in the hospital. The doctor didn't want to discuss it with you, but I guess it doesn't matter now. Clara was carrying our daughter."

Marta knew what the divorce had been about. She turned white. "Oh my God!"

"I didn't know either. I'm sure Clara knew, but she said nothing to me. I don't know if she was waiting, or if she was planning to tell me at all."

"Lou, she would have told you, you know that. That was what all the arguments were about, after all."

"I just don't know. I guess now I never will."

"I'm just flabbergasted that she never told anyone. Lou, she wasn't like that. I'm sure she planned to tell you. Maybe she was waiting for the right time."

I looked at her for a moment. "Yeah, I suppose you're right." I took another swallow.

CHAPTER 12

As things started to settle down a little, I tried to wrap up the loose ends. I placed a call to Clara's lawyer. We'd met at the funeral but we'd only exchanged a few words there. He told me that the divorce case would be dropped, but we needed to make a court appearance, so I let him work on that, telling him I was available whenever he needed me. I was surprised when he called back a couple of hours later and told me we had an appointment with the judge the following morning at ten.

After a brief court session, the judge said that though the divorce proceedings were in process, everything still reverted to me as the heir since nothing had been finalized. Clara hadn't changed beneficiaries on anything yet, so her insurance policies, 401k, and bank accounts all came to me. I needed to file documents for each one.

After talking with the judge, we went back to the lawyer's office to try to wrap up things from his end. He offered to assist me with getting the accounts switched over, but I figured I could handle that part myself. He also pointed out that Clara had given him a retainer up-front that would cover most of the costs, though there were a few more expenses. He said he would send the final bill over to the house by the end of the week, and as I got up to leave, he repeated how sorry he was that this turned out the way it did. I thanked him and headed back home to the cat.

I was surprised the following day when Angie, our realtor, called. The house had been on the market for several months, but no offers had been made and not many people were interested. She told me that a couple had gone through the house a few days ago and they'd decided to make an offer.

I sat there thinking. A few days ago I was probably at the hospital, and Clara and our daughter were still alive. Since the realtor normally contacted Clara, she had left messages on her voicemail at work, but didn't try calling me until she realized something was wrong. It was then that she'd remembered the article in the paper about the accident, and put the pieces together.

Well, the house certainly hadn't been spotless when they went through, but apparently that was not a concern for them. I was glad that Furball hadn't decided to be territorial and attack them when they came through the door. He rarely did that, but once in a while...

Angie showed up about an hour later to present the offer to me. It was pretty simple. No contingencies except inspections. No current house to sell since they lived in an apartment. They were even pre-approved for the loan, so that wouldn't be a problem.

Angie seemed a little cautious because the offering price was a few thousand less than we were asking, and she thought we could get more. But at this point, I didn't care. I signed to accept the agreement.

After she left, I sat in the living room for several hours, looking around and remembering, petting the cat, and thinking about Clara, our daughter, and all the things that might have been.

CHAPTER 13

The first thing I did when I got off the plane was find Furb. He had never flown before and he was not a happy cat. I grabbed my other bag and left the terminal, then hooked his leash to his harness so I could let him out of the crate. He seemed to feel a little better as he stopped for a moment, looking around and sniffing the air. This was different. When I opened the car door, he jumped right in. I took off the leash and after a few more sniffs, he curled up on the seat next to me, ready for the drive.

Back at the apartment, there were lots of things I needed to deal with. First, I called Ed at the office to let him know I was back in town and would come into work in a couple of days. Since it was already Wednesday, he said to just plan on Monday. Then, I needed to see the apartment manager to get her the pet deposit. It wasn't a problem, especially since she liked cats anyway. I took Furb with me to see her and he decided he liked her, too.

My to-do list had a thousand things I needed to get done—insurance forms to file, Clara's 401k to transfer over, accounts to close, and then the lawyers to deal with about the accident—but I couldn't face it yet. Since I still had a few more days off, I let it wait. I looked over at Furb, who was still investigating his new home. "Furb, how about a nice long walk?"

We used to go for walks on occasion in Chicago, but I never knew if he understood when I asked. Still, he came right over, so I put the harness and leash on him and away we went.

I took a different path than normal, heading directly downtown first to stop at Marie's. As we walked in, she immediately came around the counter to pet Furb. I think he was in heaven. "I had the rosebud delivered each day while you were gone, like you asked. Sergeant Johnson also came in a couple of times to talk. She was wondering if I knew when you would be back."

"Oh, darn, I guess I need to call her and let her know that I am back. Thanks for reminding me." I reached for my phone and called.

"Sandi, it's Lou. Just wanted to let you know I'm back in town."

"I see that. Turn around."

There she was, walking in the door of the flower shop. "Stopping in for a flower for Sara?"

Then she noticed Furb who was hiding behind me. "Ah, and who is this?" she asked. She knelt down and Furb came up. I was surprised when they touched noses.

"Seems like you know something about cats."

"Yeah, a little. It's a cop thing, we have to get along with everybody."

I got the rosebud and we walked out of the store.

"Sandi, do you have a minute? I want you to look at a picture." I pulled out my phone and scrolled through to find the one I was looking for.

She looked it over briefly. "Clara?"

"Yes, shortly after she died. Notice anything strange?"

She looked up, puzzled. "You put a rosebud on her stomach?"

I shook my head. "No, not me. The nurses had no explanation of where it came from, and they were the only ones around before I went in."

She spent a moment trying to process that, "But how could...? Wait, this makes no sense at all. You can't mean Sara?"

"Do you have a better suggestion? Who in Chicago would know about that? I told no one."

She waited for a long time before she answered. "You know, I was worried about you before you left." She paused momentarily. "Now I'm worried about both of us."

Sandi got a call and had to leave to help someone out. Furb and I continued our walk, heading over to Rose House. Furb was his normal curious self, looking around at everything and everyone, taking his time to check out all these new things.

As we got close to Rose House, however, something changed. His tail was more erect, his ears very perked up. He found something interesting, but for no reason I could see. As I opened the gate so we could walk up to the porch, he started getting a little skittish. I glanced around but saw nothing out of the ordinary. As I set the rose in front of the door, Furb started staring intently off the side of the porch, straining slightly against the leash. He meowed softly.

I looked in that direction but saw nothing. I glanced back at the cat, who was still intent on the side yard. I looked again and there she stood, holding her rose, tears running down her face.

"Hello, Sara." Again, I thought I detected a slight tilt of the head, or was it just my wishing? "Thank you for the rosebud you left for Clara. I appreciate that."

I had no idea what I was doing. She seemed mostly oblivious to me, but it seemed her focus changed. She looked at Furb, curiosity aroused, perhaps, though it was hard to tell much of anything about her. She watched him for a little while, and he watched her back, mewing softly, not afraid but interested, not moving.

He raised a paw as if he could reach out and touch her, though she was about twenty feet away. And then she slowly faded away. Furb looked around and then turned his head and turned to me as if to ask where she went.

"I don't know, boy. You know as much about this as I do."

CHAPTER 14

Luck was on my side for a change. The county held its scheduled tax deed sale about a week later, and since I had made some inquiries about Rose House, I received an email from the Assessor's office notifying me. Before receiving the email, I wasn't sure what my plans were, but once I saw that it was up for auction, I knew I wanted it.

As it turned out, there actually was another bidder for it this time, but he offered less than the outstanding taxes, while my bid was slightly higher. So I gave them my deposit check to clinch the deal. There had not been a mortgage on the house, so I got a clear deed. It was frightening how easy it was. Maybe I was supposed to have it.

The keys for the house had apparently gotten lost somewhere between the police department and the Assessor's office, so I was on my own with that, but it would be easy to find a locksmith to open it up and change locks for me. I suspected that was the least of my worries.

I started making a mental list of things I would need to deal with. The rose garden was a total mess and it was huge, so I needed help with that. I needed someone to check out the slate roof– that required a specialized skill set. Our house in Chicago had been new when Clara and I moved in, so all I'd done was plant some bushes and mow the grass. This project was a whole different beast and it would take me a while.

Probably the first thing was to find someone to clean the gutters. I hated heights, especially on three-story houses. The utilities had all been turned off for years, so I wanted to have a plumber and electrician around when they were turned on just as a precaution… didn't want to burn down the house now. I'd have to do an inspection to see what else, but I was sure the inside would need a lot of work. Maybe I could get a full-time housekeeper for a while and then switch back to once a week after the initial clean-up was done.

Leaving the auction, I stopped by and picked up my daily rosebud, then went over to drop it off and wander around the property. As I turned on Belle Chasse, I noticed a car that seemed to be following me, but not one I recognized. When I pull over in front of the house, it did the same. Sandi got out.

"Hey, Sandi, how's it going today?"

"What no smart remark about me following you? This time I even was!"

I laughed. "So what brings you out here today?"

"I moseyed by the auction this morning and saw you there, so I waited around until they auctioned off this one," she said, pointing her thumb over her shoulder at Rose House. "Thought I could offer some insights to the new owner. You planning to go in today?"

"No keys. Thought I'd take care of that first thing tomorrow morning."

"Well, then let me offer some pointers. Let's look around a bit."

I dropped the rose off on the porch and then we wandered the grounds. This was the first time I had seen the house from the sides and back, but no major problems showed up. A little more paint work was needed; one more broken window, boarded up, to get fixed. All in all, it was sound, though neglected. I hoped the inside had no big surprises in store.

We walked around the west side, shuffling through the leaves and weeds that were taking over, and I glanced over into Reeve's yard. Like the other homes on the block, he had several huge oaks that towered over a lovely grassy yard. I couldn't imagine he liked living next to this mess. Maybe he would be glad I bought it so it got cleaned up.

When we walked over to the glass conservatory, Sandi opened the door and we walked in. Since it was still morning, the sun wasn't coming in here yet and it wasn't particularly warm. A cast iron lawn table and several chairs sat around, all showing a lot of rust. The wooden side benches had lots of pots on them, with dry dead plants sticking out. I thought to myself, *yeah, this is going to be a lot of work*.

Sandi looked at me as we walked to the door that led into the house proper. "You want to go in?"

"It's unlocked?"

"Well, no, but there is a secret here." She turned the knob all the way and then bumped the door with her hip. It swung open. "Don't tell anybody about that until you get it fixed, and keep my name out of it."

Everything was dusty and musty. I wiped my finger across a small table in the hall and knocked about an inch of dust onto the floor. As I looked back, I could see our footprints on the dark hardwood flooring.

Sandi turned and stopped in front of me. "You sure you're ready for this?"

"As long as we don't find any bodies, I'm okay."

We continued along the hallway, passing a couple of doorways until we came to the center of the house. The living room was ahead of us and the dining room past that. One of the doorways we passed led into the kitchen.

All of the furniture was still there, pictures still on the walls. I looked around the large living room, surprised at how spacious it was. "Are these twelve-foot ceilings?"

"Yes, on the first floor. The other floors both have ten-foot ceilings. And there is an unfinished area at the back of the third that they used for storage."

As we went towards the front door, I noticed the wide staircase on my left that came down from the second floor and swung a little wider as it got near the bottom. "Wow, this is quite a place." I looked around, taking it all in. "Why is the furniture and everything still here?"

"Well, it was technically a crime scene for several years, so nobody could get rid of it. After that, the city took it over and they only did the absolute necessities, like boarding up the broken windows. No one wanted to be in here. They even brought someone in from out of town to fix the windows; the local guys wouldn't touch it."

I looked over the sofa and chairs and tables in the living room with their blanket of dust. Good grief, where do you start to clean up something that looks like this?

She raised her eyebrows and tilted her head. "Come on, one of the more interesting parts is over here," she said, walking towards the dining room.

This would be my first test.

She stopped again and turned around. "Umm, let me know if you see anything, okay?"

I nodded. "Nothing yet. Not even Sara outside." I grinned at her, "Hoping you'll see something?"

She glared at me.

I saw the chair turned over at one end of the dining room, right next to the table.

Sandi walked over there. "Well, you get off easy here. I suspect the blood stains will be obvious once you get the dust vacuumed up. This is where we found Stella, the mother. The back of her skull was crushed in. We later found a fireplace poker up in the study on the second floor. The blood on it matched hers."

I was glad the dust was there. I'd have to come to terms with the reality of all this soon enough, but not now.

We went into the kitchen through another doorway. Nothing was out of place here. Everything was dingy and the light coming in through the dirty windows didn't help a whole lot. I was actually glad that it was cloudy—I didn't need too much detail my first time through.

"Oh, we walked by a doorway when we came in. That leads to a bedroom and bathroom that was used as the servant's quarters. You'll need to know that later, when you start hiring people, right?"

"Dry sense of humor, Sandi. I don't expect to need that one at all. Maybe I should move in there first until I get the rest of the place cleaned up."

"Come on upstairs. I think you might change your mind."

As we got to the top of the stairs, she turned right and then went into the first door. This was the study, situated so that it looked out over the front garden and the street.

The desk in the middle of the room was beautiful, mahogany perhaps, and quite large. I looked at the floor-to-ceiling bookcases on either side, still filled with books, many in leather bindings. I started to walk over to look out the window and then stopped dead. Even in the dim light, I saw dark stains on the wall next to the window and on the ceiling above it. A chill ran down my spine. "This is where the father died, right?"

"Yes. All the evidence we found indicated that Harper just put the gun in his mouth while sitting in the chair. He left a glass sitting on the desk that still had some bourbon in it. It was fairly straightforward to determine that he was the one responsible, but we never found a motive."

I shivered briefly and walked out of the room.

"Hey, you okay?"

"Yeah, though I thought it would be a little easier than this."

"We don't have to do this now, you know. Might be better when you get the power turned on and you get some light in here."

"No, it's okay, let's keep going."

We turned left and looked into the two bedrooms that faced each other at the end of the hall. In each, the beds were neatly made and everything looked normal, but needed a thorough cleaning.

"These were the boys' bedrooms. Max had the room at the front of the house, Owen had the one at the back."

"The ones who were never found?"

"Yes."

"Did they actually have a housekeeper when this all happened?"

"Interesting question. Yes, they had a live-in housekeeper that had been with them for over five years. We talked to her, of course. Apparently, there were some arguments that she'd heard between Harper and Stella a few weeks before all this happened, but she never could tell what they were about, just raised voices from other parts of the house.

"Then, about a week before the murders, Harper fired her. Told her to take all her stuff and get out of the house. He gave her no reason, paid her up to date and threw her out. It came as a total surprise to her. You can try to talk to her if you want. She works for Reeve next door now, but she doesn't like anyone bringing it up anymore and doesn't like to talk about it. She was very upset when the news came out. She helped raise the children and was very close to them all, according to neighbors. She answered our questions, but it was hard for her."

"How did she come to work for Reeve?"

"They had been looking for someone for a while and asked her if she knew anyone that was responsible and interested in a live-in position, but then all this took place. They'd known her for years and she'd always done a great job with the house and the kids loved her. With no job and no place of her own, she just moved her clothes next door and started working for them. Besides, Reeve said Harper was acting odd right before this... very quiet, only nodded to the neighbors and stayed inside more than normal."

"Was Reeve ever a suspect?"

"Not really. The Dylans were a little standoffish, so they weren't close friends, but they spoke on occasion." Sandi smiled slightly. "In spite of his faults, I can't imagine Reeve would kill the family just to get their maid."

"Yeah, probably not."

The next bedroom was across from the study. The wallpaper was a light yellow with flowers, and there were dolls everywhere, along with a few posters of animated movie characters from seven years ago. "Sara's room?"

Sandi nodded. "We found her on the bed, which was made up, but the pillow was missing, just like you see it here. We tried to leave as much alone as possible in case someone noticed something that would give us a clue. And, of course, we took pictures of pretty much the whole place."

I shook my head, thinking about her crying in the garden. Why? What had happened?

The next bedroom had pastel print wallpaper and a bed that was low to the floor. "This was Libby's room. Drea, the housekeeper, said they'd just moved her out of the crib since she was trying to climb out and they'd put the bed in here. She was lying on the bed, cold, just like Sara. Forensic reports indicated they were both suffocated. The extra pillow that was in here matched the bedspread in Sara's room and we believe he used it to kill them both."

The final door at the end of the hallway opened to a large master bedroom that ran from the front of the house to the back if you counted the bathroom along the back wall. Again, this one had wallpaper, in a more formal striped pattern that coordinated with the drapes and bedspread.

After looking around for a moment, I glanced over at Sandi. "I didn't think the bedrooms were normally so large in houses that were built, what, a hundred years ago?"

"One hundred thirteen, to be precise. And you're right, it is a little unusual but not unheard of. Stella had this little sitting area set up at one end of the room that overlooked the front yard. Everything here is pretty much as we found it... beds made, neat as a pin. We looked through closets and drawers pretty extensively, but found nothing of interest."

I looked around the room at the canopied bed and the nice chairs in the sitting area, wondering. "Clarify something for me, Sandi, would you? I get all the furniture and stuff in the house, too?"

She smiled at me. "You bought it, you got it. Fully furnished except for a few items we took for evidence, and you can probably get those back. We couldn't find anyone else to give it to anyway. I guess it's just your lucky day, so to speak."

I grimaced at her and went back to look over the bathroom. Very nice, though somewhat outdated, but it matched the style of the house well. "Is this original to the house?"

"Can't answer that one. It wasn't relevant to the investigation."

As we walked back down the hallway, I noticed a closed door that we almost bypassed. I turned the knob and it opened onto another staircase that went down to the back of the house and came out between the kitchen and the maid's quarters.

"So, there's also a third floor. What's up there?"

"Storage in the back, a playroom for the kids in the front, where the noise wouldn't bother their parents when they entertained, I guess. A couple of spare bedrooms. Nothing that held any interest for us, though we went through them to make sure."

"Just curious, Sandi, how much time did you spend in here after the murders?"

"Way too much. Some days when we were getting nowhere, I'd come over and just sit in one of the chairs or wander the house, hoping for something to pop up." She looked at her watch. "I probably should get going, but let's see if Reeve is around first. I'll introduce you to him."

"Maybe we'll get off on a better foot this time."

CHAPTER 15

Sandi knocked on the front door of the Marchant home as I enjoyed the peacefulness of the neighborhood. I could get used to this... I certainly hoped so since I'd bought the house next door.

A thin, middle-aged woman wearing a black and white maid's uniform answered the door. "Oh, Sergeant Johnson. Please come in. I'm assuming you're looking for Mr. Marchant?"

"Well, yes, but first, Drea, this is Lou Navelliere. You'll probably see a lot of him since he just bought the house next door."

She looked shocked. "Rose House?"

"Yes, someone finally bought it."

She looked at me gravely, concerned. "Oh, I do hope you don't have any problems with it, Mr. Navelliere. It was a beautiful house at one point in time."

I smiled at her, trying to ease into this. "Oh, I think I'll be fine there, though there is a lot of work needed."

From the hallway, we heard "You can say that again" as Reeve walked into the room. "How are you, Sandi?"

"Fine, sir. Just thought I would introduce your new neighbor while we are here. I think you have seen each other before."

Reeve looked like he was assessing me. "Yes, we have." Then, addressing me, "I think I might have overreacted when you showed up last time. Let me apologize." He extended his hand.

"No need. From what Sandi told me, you had good cause for concern with the other people that hung around before."

"Well, you're the first one that ever considered buying the house. The rest were just interested in making the news headlines, near as I could tell."

Smiling at him, I said "That's certainly not my intent. I prefer to keep a low profile."

"Well, maybe it will all work out for the best. That house needs a lot of work, though, as I'm sure you noticed."

"Yes, I did. In fact, I have a favor to ask of you if you don't mind. I'm from out of town and now I find myself needing a temporary gardener, plumber, electrician, etc. If there is anyone you could recommend, I would appreciate it."

"Well, sure, I can do that. I'll put that together for you and put it in your mailbox. How would that be?"

"That would be great. I need to get rolling on it."

"Any idea when you might be moving in?"

"Not yet, there is a tremendous amount of cleaning that is needed. I want to replace appliances and things, and I need to make sure the electrical, plumbing and heating work all right after sitting for so long. Then I'll do a general inspection to make sure there's nothing else to take care of."

Reeve nodded thoughtfully. "Sounds like you'll need some help getting it cleaned out, too. Is that right?"

"Yeah, I'd like to hire somebody to help with that, even if it's only temporary."

Reeve laughed again. "I think you might find you want more than temporary. It's a big house and they take a lot of work. I'll ask Drea if she knows anyone who would be willing to help, though I suspect a lot of people would turn it down because of its history."

"I would appreciate that immensely. And please call me Lou."

"Sure thing, and I'm Reeve." He paused a moment and we turned to go. "Oh, by the way, do you have any idea yet when you plan to start working on it?"

"You'll see me around quite a bit for a while, but I don't have any date in mind yet. As soon as possible. As you said, there's a lot to do there, so I want to get started."

He shook my hand again. "Let me know if there is anything else I can do. I'll get those names and phone numbers to you, probably tomorrow."

"Thanks again, Reeve."

CHAPTER 16

On Monday I took the afternoon off. The locksmith met me at Rose House and proceeded to change all of the outside door locks, including the one to the basement that I hadn't thought about and the one to the conservatory. It took him several hours and a trip back to his business for something, and then he left me with a handful of keys, all matched. But after that, I wasn't sure what I planned to do, since the utilities were still off.

I wandered around the house to more thoroughly check out the parts I'd missed before. Since it was a sunny day, it was easier to see things, but that also meant I saw some things better than I would have liked, such as the blood stains in the den. Or was I going to call it a study? Or a library? Time would tell. No real surprises came up as I wandered through, but I took the time to open windows and let some air through the house. It needed it.

Then I remembered Reeve's offer. Sure enough, in the mailbox was a note from him and a list of just about every type of service I could need: roofer, carpenter, handyman, gardener, painter, pest control, car mechanic. Based on the list, I got the impression that Reeve didn't do much himself around his house. The only thing missing was a housekeeper, but that part I could handle. So I sat down at the foot of the main stair in the living room and started making phone calls. The first one was to the utility companies to get water, electric and gas service. Then I called to get a plumber and electrician and I was fortunate enough to get them to come out on Friday when the services were being turned on, though it took a little persuading. Since the house had been sitting empty for so long, I figured the electric would probably be fine unless squirrels had chewed the wires, but I was very skeptical of the condition of the plumbing and I certainly didn't want a flood, especially since I had no idea where to find the water shutoff.

Then, I got to make the call that I really wanted to make: the gardener. I'm not sure why, but I wanted to get the gardens cleaned out and pruned back as soon as possible. Maybe it was because that was where I usually saw Sara. I thought of it as a kind of tribute to her to put things back the way they used to be as soon as possible. When I reached him, the gardener knew exactly what it looked like since he worked next door once a week, so we discussed what I needed and he offered suggestions on things he could do and when. Since I wanted to be there, at least when they got started, we set that up for Saturday, the first day he had time. His guess was that it would take three of them a day or two for general cleanup, weed-pulling, and mulching, and then he would work by himself for another three to four days for the pruning and whatever else we agreed on. I was feeling better about the house already, and looking forward to getting it presentable.

Even though I was excited about the prospects, I couldn't think of anything else to do around here for the afternoon so I closed the windows I'd opened earlier. At least the house wasn't nearly as stuffy as before. I was on the third floor closing the last one when I noticed an older Toyota pull up across the street, with rust spots and a few dents. A young woman got out and looked around, then headed towards my yard. I couldn't tell what she looked like from up here, but I started downstairs to see what she wanted.

She got to the door before I got down there and I heard her knock loudly on the door frame as I rounded the corner for the last flight of stairs. I yelled "Hold on" and trotted down the last flight to open the door.

The woman in front of me was in her late teens or early twenties, with dark brown hair and blue eyes. Her smile was warm and she seemed very confident. Her skin had a slight mocha tone that enhanced her eye color. If it wasn't for the car, I would have wondered what she was trying to sell.

"Are you Mr. Navelliere?" she asked, peeking past me into the house.

"Yes, how can I help you?"

"I overheard my Aunt Drea say that you bought this house and were looking for someone to help clean it up, though she also told my mother that she didn't want anyone she knew going in here."

This was a little confusing. "Your aunt is the one who works next door that used to work here?"

"Yes, she works for Mr. Marchant now."

"Why is she saying people should stay away?"

She smiled awkwardly. "She says the house is evil and that those terrible things that happened might happen again, but I don't believe in that kind of thing. Do you?"

"Well, it is true that terrible things happened here, but they won't happen again if I have anything to say about it. What is your name?"

"Oh, I'm sorry. My name is Adrienne, but everybody calls me Addie." She paused, embarrassed. "You must think I have no manners at all."

I smiled. "No worse than me. I'm Lou Navelliere." We shook hands briefly. "But I am a little confused as to why you are here after what your aunt said."

"I was hoping you'd hire me to help clean up. I've helped Aunt Drea a few times next door, so I know what kinds of things need to be done."

I opened the door further and motioned her to come in. "Well, in all honesty, the place is filthy and it's big, so it's going to take quite a while to clean up, as you can tell."

She glanced around, looking a little stunned. "Oh my, it *is* a mess!"

"I can show you around the place if you would like, but I have a question first. Do you believe in ghosts?"

She raised one eyebrow and gave me a strange look. "Well, I've never seen one. Have you?"

"Maybe. Does that bother you?"

Addie paused for a moment as if making up her mind, then decided. "No. If they leave me alone, I'll leave them alone." She gave me another of her bright smiles.

"Okay, so one more question. How is Drea going to react when she finds out you are working here?"

She lowered her eyes. "I was hoping she wouldn't find out, at least for a while. Is that all right?"

I nodded slowly. "I can do that, but with her next door..." I let my voice trail off.

She looked up, paused for a moment, then shrugged. "I guess I'll just deal with that when it comes to it."

"It just seems a little odd that your aunt said not to come here, but here you are anyway, and you want to keep it a secret."

This time she looked more embarrassed. "I'm sorry, it's just that I really need a job, so when I heard about this..."

"And you understand that this is only a temporary position until things get cleaned up and I get my stuff moved in?"

"Well, that will be all right. Like I said, I need a job."

"Where did you work last?"

"Henry's Fried Chicken, down on Main Street. I liked it there okay, but they wanted me to work nights and that's a problem with my daughter. My mother watches her during the day, but it just wasn't working very well when I worked nights."

She was young, so this surprised me a little. "How old is your daughter?"

"She's four, but as long as I work days, my mom is fine watching her."

So far, I'd heard nothing that concerned me. Granted, I couldn't check with her aunt for a reference, but I was only looking for someone to help me clean up for a few weeks or so. "Would you like to look around the house so you can see what you're getting into?"

"Sure, I'd like that."

I paused for a moment. "Would you be okay working weekends?"

"Yes, that would be fine, too. As long as it's not nights, any day will work."

I showed her the downstairs without going into the details about what she might find. Then a thought occurred to me. "Do you remember anything about when the killings took place here?"

"Sure, everyone in town talked about it. I was a little young and didn't pay much attention, but you couldn't go anywhere without hearing about it."

"How did your aunt take it, if you don't mind my asking?"

"Aunt Drea was very upset. She'd worked here for years and she always said she loved those kids like they were her own. I remember her crying in our living room when she found out they were dead. She just had no idea how that could have happened."

I considered this as we walked up the stairs to the second floor. First, we went to the boys' rooms.

"The boys that were never found?"

"Yes," I answered, but I was getting cautious. I knew I needed help to clean the place up and didn't want to scare her off.

In the den, she noticed the blood stains right away. "Is this where Mr. Dylan killed himself?" she asked, shivering a little.

"Yes, it is. I'll hire a cleaning company to take care of this room, then get the wallpaper taken down and have it painted."

She looked at me defiantly. "Nothing here I can't take care of. I'm not afraid of this, Mr. Navelliere."

I smiled a little, trying to lighten things up a little. "I think you have more courage than I do about this."

She grinned at me, seeming more comfortable, and then we went down to the master bedroom. "Well, this will be a very nice place once I get it cleaned up!"

I noticed her choice of wording. She had more confidence than I'd expected under the circumstances, but I found it amusing. As we walked out of the master, we came to Libby's room and I felt myself getting nervous. Every time I thought about Sara's room, I got nervous, and that was next on the list.

Addie got quiet as we looked around the baby's room. "She was so young when she died. Never really had a chance, did she?"

I shook my head and we went on. As we walked into Sara's room, I saw the girl standing there, holding her rose, watching. She wasn't crying this time, but she had the same slightly curious expression on her face as she looked from me to Addie. I froze, said nothing, not knowing whether Addie saw her or not, or how she might react.

But Addie looked around the room as if nothing was out of the ordinary. As she turned to go, she saw me standing by the door, frozen. "Are you all right, Mr. Navelliere?" She tried following my gaze but apparently saw nothing.

I shook myself, trying to get my composure back. "I'll be fine. Thanks, Addie."

We toured the third floor after that, but I was shaken and said very little. I got occasional curious glances from Addie, but ignored them.

As we arrived back at the front door, she looked at me closely. "Mr. Navelliere, did you see something up there, in Sara's room?"

I paused a long time before answering, but it wouldn't be right to not let her know what she was getting into. "Yes. Sara was there."

Addie's eyes got wide and she stared at me. I thought to myself, "*Well, I won't blame her for leaving,*" knowing that she would.

She took her time, then said, "Would you want me to start this weekend?"

CHAPTER 17

I wasn't very productive at work the rest of the week. It was like I was going through the motions but getting nothing accomplished. Since Ed, my boss, knew much of what was happening in my life, he gave me some leeway and also let me take Friday off to get the utilities connected. He was glad to hear that I'd bought a house since it meant I was obviously planning to stay, but when he heard it was Rose House he got quiet and said nothing more about it.

Most of my time was spent making more mental lists of things to do. The refrigerator and dishwasher would definitely go, but I couldn't realistically order replacements until the house had electric and water. Plus, it made no sense to try to get that done until the kitchen was cleaned up at the very least. Maybe it made more sense to wait until I was close to moving in. At this point, it seemed like that would be months away.

In the middle of my distractions on Wednesday afternoon, my cell phone rang. The man identified himself as Jim Fleet, from the insurance company representing the 'other person involved in the accident with your wife.' I'd known this was coming sooner or later.

"So what can I do for you, Mr. Fleet?"

"Well, Mr. Navelliere, first let me say that I'm sorry for your loss. I understand how difficult losing someone close to you can be."

"Umm, yeah, thanks." I was annoyed already and wasn't about to make this easier for him.

"I know this is a hard time for you and so we thought it would be best if we get the insurance claim process settled as quickly as possible. For many people, that helps them put the difficulty behind them and move on with their life. We have an offer here that I would like to go over with you, and I think you will find it quite generous."

He was too smooth and too glib. "Jim, let me have your contact information and I'll have my lawyer get in touch with you."

"Sir, I'm sure you realize that bringing a lawyer into this process will take a substantial portion of the settlement out of your pocket and might extend the process immensely. I was hoping to settle this without the necessity of getting others involved and potentially going to court over this issue, since it is pretty clear what happened."

"You mean that your client, with multiple DUI convictions and who was drunk at the time of the accident, killed my wife through no fault of hers?"

He hesitated for just a moment. "Well, I don't think there is anything to be gained here by trying to place blame. We just want to settle the claim so that you can move on."

"Let's see. Your client was drunk at the time of the accident according to the police report, which put his blood alcohol level at twice the legal limit. Then he illegally attempted to pass my wife's car when she slowed down to make a left turn into our driveway, with her turn signal on at the time, as also shown in the police report, and you don't want to place blame? Either give me your contact information or I'll hang up. My lawyer can find you."

"Sir, maybe I didn't make myself clear. We're just trying—"

I hung up before he got any further. They weren't getting off that easily if I had anything to say about it.

I was still sitting at my desk, fuming, when Ed stuck his head in.

"You okay, Lou? You look ready to put someone out of their misery."

I took a deep breath. "Sorry, just got a call from the insurance company representing the guy who killed my wife. They'd like to settle this as soon as possible so 'I can move on.'"

"Oh, God. This just makes it all the harder to get through. They just want to get you when you're vulnerable before you've had a chance to think things through."

I looked at him and nodded. "Yep."

"Look, it's already after four, so get out of here and try to cool down a little."

"Thanks, Ed. I know I already missed a lot of work. I'll make it up to you."

He smiled. "It happens to all of us for different reasons. I was gone over a month when we had our last son because of some of his issues. You're just dealing with different circumstances. Go on, get out of here."

CHAPTER 18

I got to Rose House about seven on Saturday morning.

The utility companies had come by the previous day, along with the plumber and electrician. The plumber found a couple of issues with leaking faucets, but they were pretty simple for him to fix. He warned me that more problems could crop up in the next couple of weeks, but after that things should settle down.

The electrician determined that the outlet to the refrigerator was fine, so it must be the refrigerator that was dead. He said the air conditioning unit would need servicing, but it ran. Plus, he found a bunch of light bulbs that were out. Overall, it could have turned out a lot worse.

As I unlocked the front door, I heard a cheerful voice behind me. "Good morning, Mister Navelliere!"

I turned around and smiled at Addie. She wore an old pair of jeans and a sweat-shirt and looked ready to get to work. I looked out into the street. "What, no car today?"

She grinned and glanced away for a moment. "If I leave that car sitting here all day, Aunt Drea is surely going to come over and give me a piece of her mind. I got a ride over today. How's the house doing?"

"Well, we have water and electric, so I guess we're in business. Plus, I picked up a vacuum and some cleaning supplies. You let me know what other things you need and I'll get them for you. And please call me Lou."

"By the way, have we had any visitors this morning?"

I knew what she was talking about right away, so I shook my head. "No, I haven't seen Sara since you were over here before."

"Did you ever see any of the others?"

"No, just her."

We walked into the foyer and she put her hands on her hips and looked around. "So where do you want me to start?"

I smiled. "It is a big project, and I'm wondering that myself. I think the first thing we should do is get the bathroom on the first floor cleaned up, then work on the kitchen, and after that maybe the downstairs bedroom."

"I like the idea of getting the bathroom ready first!" She grinned at me. "Where is the stuff you got?"

I showed her where I had stacked things on the kitchen counter and she grabbed some of the cleaners and went off.

I was about to measure for the new refrigerator when the doorbell rang.

Addie called from the kitchen, "You want me to get that?"

"I got it. I think it's Kwan Ying and his gardening crew. I'll be outside getting them started."

Kwan had his truck parked on the street and his two workers were unloading wheelbarrows from on top of the mulch he'd brought. Kwan was thin and wiry, probably in his mid-forties with a little gray hair starting to show at his temples. He and his assistants all wore khaki shirts with 'Kwan's Gardening, we can do it!' on them. "Good morning! I have my two nephews, Matthew and Abraham, to help, and we are ready to go."

"Pleased to meet you in person, Kwan." I shook his hand. "Matthew and Abraham, okay, got it."

He rolled his eyes and grinned. "Don't even ask. Where do you want us to start?"

We wandered briefly through the yard, discussing what he thought needed to be done first, and decided to start in front and work towards the back. That way it would look better from the street right away. For the dead roses, he planned to put a marker by them and I'd tell him what kind to get to replace them. Since he'd worked here before and also worked for Reeve, he knew more about what it needed than I did, so I let him get started.

"Oh, you can put your truck in the driveway if you want."

"You're not going anywhere?"

"My car is the one on the street right in front of your truck."

With that Kwan went to move the truck while his nephews fired up blowers and started blowing off the leaves and the occasional sheet of paper that had accumulated. I had to admit, they weren't wasting any time.

After watching them work for a few minutes, I remembered that I wanted to check out the garage, so I walked back there. On the way, I waved at Reeve, who pulled out of his driveway.

The side door to my garage was unlocked so I went in to look around. It was an older building, but probably not original to the house, with three separate doors, and they were the newer metal kind, each with its own opener. I knew those weren't around when the house was built, so there must have been some changes and upgrades over the years.

To my surprise, two cars were parked in the garage. The space behind the third door was filled with random pieces of stuff, much of which I didn't recognize.

The car closest to the house was a Lincoln SUV about ten years old, black. It was dirty but it looked like it might clean up pretty well, if it still ran. I guessed that was probably the Dylans everyday car.

The other was an old Cadillac, probably from the early sixties, also covered in dust and grime. It was long and white with fins, of course, but looked like it would be practically showroom new once it got cleaned up. Looking in through the closed windows, I noticed the leather seats were in perfect condition. I wasn't going to start to work on these until Furb and I got moved in and the house was usable.

Out of curiosity, I hit the wall buttons for the garage doors and was surprised when all three of them opened, though with some squeaking and groaning in the process. The handyman would be able to get them lubricated and maybe that was all they needed. It sure made it look less gloomy. I closed it up and went back to the house with more projects to add to the list.

CHAPTER 19

By six o'clock the gardeners were ready to call it a day and the light was starting to fade. All the dry leaves were gone and you could actually see the flagstone walkways that meandered through the yard, and the benches placed here and there to sit and enjoy the flowers. I thought that maybe I should add a fountain or two, particularly in the side yards, but again, that project would wait until I moved in.

A lot of the weeds near the street were already gone and they had started mulching and sweeping things up, so that part of it looked pretty good. A lot remained to be done in the back, but they were returning the next day to continue.

After they left I found Addie cleaning up the kitchen. "Still here, huh?"

She looked a little tired, but she still smiled as she put some stuff in one of the cabinets. "Sure thing. You want me to keep working?"

"You look a little tired, so why don't you call it quits for the day."

"Well, let me show you what's done."

I had seen the bathroom earlier and she had done an amazing job on it, but she wanted to point out that the floor was scrubbed along with pretty much everything else in the room. She had also gotten rid of the cobwebs and wiped down the wallpaper. If the rest of the house turned out this well, I was going to be very happy.

"Addie, you've done a wonderful job here today. I really appreciate how much effort you put into this." She'd been a dynamo all day, only slowing down late in the afternoon.

In addition to the bathroom, she had vacuumed the foyer, kitchen, and hallway so we weren't tracking dirt back into the parts she had cleaned. Then she showed me what she had done in the kitchen, cleaning off counters and dusting out cabinets.

"Mr. Lou, as soon as you get the new dishwasher put in I'll run all of the dishes through it, unless you want me to do them by hand."

"No, it can wait. I'm not moving in quite yet and I want the kitchen fully working before I do. I'm more interested in cleaning rooms than washing dishes. And you can drop the mister, just call me Lou."

"Well, I made a list of some things I need to keep going. Seems like I used up half the paper towels already. By the way, which room is next after the kitchen?"

We walked down the hall and I showed her the maid's room. "Is this where Drea stayed?"

"Well sure! She said at first she was just coming in a couple of times a week, but then she moved in here and stayed here in this room for the last four or five years."

"Well, once you get this cleaned up, I might consider moving in here while we work on the rest of the house."

"When there's such a nice big bedroom upstairs?"

I paused for a moment. "Well, that one is closer to Sara's room."

"Oh, there is that."

"But sooner or later I'll just have to face it."

Addie smiled. "Same time in the morning?"

"Sure, that will be good."

As she turned towards the front door, she said, "And thanks for the pizzas for lunch. I know the gardeners were surprised by that too."

CHAPTER 20

Kwan and his nephews were hard at work when I got there around 7:15, so I just waved to them as I headed up to the porch. Addie sat there waiting for me to unlock the door, but all she said was "Good morning, Lou. Is it still all right if I call you that?"

"Sure, that's fine," I said as I opened the door. "Come with me for a minute."

We walked into the kitchen and I opened the cabinet above the stove, which she hadn't cleaned out yet. I grabbed a key from the little box I had put there and handed it to her. "Here. In case I'm late next time, you'll be able to get in."

She seemed pleasantly surprised but said nothing and stuck it in her pocket.

"How's your daughter this morning?"

She smiled again; she did that a lot. "Well, she was still asleep when I left, but she's fine. She's even happy that I have a job."

"Is that because *you* are happy you have a job? Kids pick up on things like that."

"Could be."

I hadn't asked before, but was interested. "So how old were you when you had her?"

Addie blushed. "Well, aren't you the curious one!"

"Never mind, none of my business. Sorry I asked."

"I had her two months after I graduated from high school. I'm twenty-two now and so much wiser! Must have been all that reading I did."

I laughed at her mocking herself. "And what about her father?"

"Somehow he seemed to disappear right after he heard I was pregnant."

I looked at her, reassessing. She had been through a lot in a short time and was still doing her best to get through. I realized she probably knew more about 'life lessons' than I did, even though I was about ten years her senior. "Oh, sorry I brought it up."

"So is the plan for today still the same—finish up some in the kitchen and then work on the downstairs bedroom?"

"That sounds good. I'll be gone for a while. I need to get a new refrigerator and dishwasher so I'm going to run to the hardware store."

"Are you planning to replace the washer and dryer, too?"

"Hmm, I hadn't planned quite that far ahead, but that's a good idea. I'll see what I can find."

"You might check out Gary's Appliances up on Alberon. He gives people a pretty good deal, and with everything you're buying I'm sure he'll be happy to work with you."

"A relative of yours?"

She laughed again. "No, but my mom bought a few things from him and he treated her pretty fair."

"I suppose I should get a new microwave too, huh?"

"Well, the one on the counter doesn't do anything except turn on the inside light."

"Okay, I'm on it."

"Oh, Lou, what do you want me to work on after the bedroom?"

"Well, the rest of the downstairs. Start with the dining room, I guess."

That got a grimace, so I guessed she knew what had happened there. "Sooner or later I just have to face it, right?"

***

About four hours later I returned to the house after making arrangements to get a truckload of appliances delivered on Tuesday. Gary was very helpful and looked over all of the measurements I'd brought, offering a lot of suggestions. I chuckled to myself when he pointed out that such a nice house 'really deserves nice appliances'. On the other hand, his prices were better than I'd expected and then he threw in free delivery and installation.

When I walked into the house, I found Addie staring at the carpet in the dining room, hands on her hips. There were obvious dark stains on it where Stella had been killed.

"Problem, Addie?"

"Well, these stains sure won't come out with the vacuum. I'm not sure what I can do with this carpet."

I thought about suggesting that she ask Drea, but I knew that would not make her happy. "Do you know any place that can clean it?"

She thought for a moment. "Well, I think so, but they're pretty expensive."

I shrugged. "That's okay, I think I'm headed for bankruptcy anyway," I joked.

"No sir, not until you pay me first!" she said with another smile.

We each grabbed an end of the table and moved it off the rug far enough that we could roll it up.

I looked at her again. "Are you going to tell me where to take it?"

She thought for a moment. "If you want, I could just pick it up tomorrow and take it over to Madison's. I do have a key now."

"Addie, you can't move it by yourself. It's heavy and awkward."

"My sister is off work tomorrow, so I'll bring her. But if you don't want me to, that's fine."

"If you want to take care of it, it's okay with me."

We moved the carpet close to the front door so she wouldn't have to carry it very far, then I asked her, "Any visitors while I was gone?"

She made a funny face at me. "I don't know why you see Sara but I can't. That doesn't seem right."

"Are you sure you want to?"

Serious expression. "Well, no, not really."

"Be careful what you wish for."

CHAPTER 21

On Tuesday morning I mentioned to Ed that I needed to take half a day of vacation because of the appliance deliveries.

He looked at me, nodding. "You know, there's a meeting of the Rotary Club at eleven o'clock and I need to deliver some papers to the president. If you could do that for me, I would appreciate it. Then you can stay for the meeting and socialize afterward, or not. You know how these business meetings go; it could last all afternoon." He grinned at me.

"You know, Ed, you're being much too nice to me. Is there something I should be worried about?"

He laughed. "Just trying to keep my people happy."

Well, it turned out that he gave me no 'papers' at all, but he did hand me an empty envelope to make it look like I was leaving on business. He sent me off, without any directions on where the meeting was. I stopped at Marie's to pick up a rosebud and went on over to Rose House. Addie had found a nice vase that she'd cleaned up and the prior day I'd put the rose in there on the dining room table. As I thought about it later, that might have been a mistake, since it was where Sara's mother had died. I wish I had thought of that earlier.

I walked into the house and went directly to the dining room. Sitting in the middle of the table was the vase, right where I'd left it. No rose. Well, I guess that meant Sara had found it, so I put in some fresh water, added the new rosebud, and put it back on the table.

The appliance people actually showed up just as I finished doing that, so I was glad I got there early. They brought a good-sized moving van with two people and then a car that followed with two more.

"Did you bring the whole staff for this project?"

The crew manager laughed at that. "With everything we need to get installed, I thought it would be better to have two crews so we get things done quicker for you. Even so, it's going to take a while."

I showed them into the kitchen and then the small laundry room that was between it and the maid's quarters.

"Mr. Navelliere, do you want us to dispose of the old appliances for you? There's no charge for that."

"Sure, that's perfect." Then the doorbell rang so I left them to do their job.

I opened the door for Sandi and invited her in.

"You sure got the gardens cleaned up fast... it's looking really good." She glanced around the foyer and living room. "The rest of the house is coming along pretty well too."

I was about to show her around when I noticed Addie's Toyota pulling into the driveway with one end of a rug sticking out the back window. I found it interesting that she drove in until the house blocked the view of her car from Reeve's house.

"Come on out, Sandi, and I'll introduce you to the young woman who is turning this place into something livable again."

As we neared the car, Addie got out and turned to us with a surprised expression. "Sergeant Johnson, good to see you again!"

"Hello, Adrienne. Lou was just telling me what a nice job you were doing cleaning the place up."

This confused me. "You two know each other?"

Sandi smiled. "Small town, you know."

Addie put one hand on her hip. "Sergeant Johnson helped out my mother with some problems a couple of months back. You got to watch out for her, she's nicer than she looks."

Sandi laughed. "I'm not quite sure how I should take that, Adrienne, but thanks."

She shook her head. "Well, it didn't come out quite the way I meant it, but you know we appreciate everything you did for us. You know Mr. Navelliere?"

Sandi nodded. "Yeah, we've run into each other a few times."

"Reeve?" she asked.

"You don't miss a thing, do you?"

I shook my head. "Is the carpet cleaned already?"

She nodded. "Yep, the stain is all gone. I'm not sure how they did it, but it looks nice now."

Sandi looked over at me. "You want the front end or the back end?"

We carried it into the house while Addie held the door open for us, then went into the dining room.

Johnson immediately noticed the rose in the vase. "Still keeping Marie's in business, I see."

"Of course. One a day. And every day they disappear."

She glanced over at Addie as if she weren't sure how much the girl knew.

Addie looked back at her and said, "But it's funny, I never get to see Sara, just Lou."

She looked at me. "Still hallucinating, huh?"

I grimaced and tilted my head. "Old habits are hard to change." Then I looked over at Addie. "By the way, what are you doing here today?"

"Oh, I just wanted to get the carpet back as soon as possible so I can finish the dining room and move on to the next one. Don't worry, you don't have to pay me for this."

"Well, Addie, no wonder you need a job if you work for nothing!"

She frowned at me. "Are the appliances going in? Can I go see?"

So, we all wandered into the kitchen. The old refrigerator sat in the middle of the floor while they ran a water line for the new one, which was right beside it. I heard noises coming from the laundry room too, and one of the guys wheeled the old washer out and headed for the door.

Addie offered a few suggestions to the installers, so Sandi and I walked back into the foyer.

"Do you still see Sara?"

"Every once in a while. I saw her up in her bedroom when I was showing Addie the house, but I haven't seen her since. Still, the roses disappear every day."

"You sure it's not some kind of prank?"

"Well, the last one was taken from the dining room table. The house was locked and all of the locks are changed."

She nodded. "Well, I should be going. I just wanted to see how things were coming. The house is looking much better already." As I walked with her out to her car, she added, "Adrienne is quite a girl, reliable and trustworthy. I'm glad you found her."

CHAPTER 22

When I walked back into the house I found Addie in the maid's quarters and we discussed the next items on the agenda. "I wasn't planning on redecorating in here until later, but I think we should at least replace the mattress and get new sheets and stuff. What do you think?"

"The mattress seems okay from what I can tell, and I found some sheets and stuff we can use, if you would like. They're in the linen closet."

I shook my head. "You know, as much as I love this house, I don't want to use any of the same mattresses or linens. I'd rather replace them. Call me superstitious if you want, but it would just seem weird. And I guess I'll be giving away all of the clothing. Is there someplace around here I can take it?"

Addie nodded. "There are a couple of places, and I can run them over sometime during the day if you'd like. Do you want me to go through everything first?"

"That sounds like a good idea. The police probably checked it all when they went through years ago, though I can't imagine there is anything of interest in any of it. After you get this room cleaned up you can start on that. It should make cleaning out the bedrooms easier when you get to them."

"You know, I'll need some more supplies pretty soon, too."

"What, you wore out the vacuum cleaner already?"

She laughed. "I'll make you a list."

"Oh, one particular favor for me."

She just looked at me, waiting.

"I noticed some fancy glasses in the china hutch in the dining room that would work well for my Scotch. Can you wash up a couple of those? No hurry. Oh, and I guess with the refrigerator here I can get some soda and beer at least, so add that to the list. If there's anything specific you want me to get for you, put that on there too.

"I'm going next door to see if Reeve is home. I need to talk to him."

As it turned out, Reeve was walking out his back door towards the garage when I came over.

"You know, Lou, you made a lot of progress already. Someone's always over there working on something, and the gardens look pretty good. It'll be nice to see the roses in bloom again this summer. Did you find someone to help you clean up over there?"

"Yes, I did. She's pretty high-energy, so a lot is getting done on the inside too." I didn't want to say too much so word didn't get back to Drea.

Reeve gave me a skeptical look. "Would you like me to send Drea over to give her some pointers?"

I had the distinct feeling that he had seen Addie, and since she had helped at his house a few times, probably recognized her right away. "No, that will be okay, she knows what she is doing."

He smiled. "I thought you might say that. If you change your mind, let me know."

"There is one thing I need your advice on. I need the name of a lawyer I can trust to help me with an insurance claim. Know a good one?"

"Sandi mentioned something about your wife. Is that what this is about?"

"Yeah, the insurance guy that called me was pretty condescending and pushy. I want some professional help on this one."

"Good idea. Come on into the house with me, I have a business card for the lawyer we use. He's always been fair and above board with us. I'm pretty sure he handles cases like this. If not, he can refer you to someone who does."

He gave me the card and I thanked him. As we walked out, I said "Hi" to Drea, but she only nodded politely. I wondered if she knew her niece was working next door, but I sure wasn't going to bring it up.

When I walked back into my house Addie sat on the couch in the living room, finishing up her list. She was near the end of the second page.

As I looked out the window, I noticed the old washer and dryer loaded into the appliance truck. The old refrigerator was already there, too, so I went into the kitchen to check on the progress.

"Mr. Navelliere, we're just about done here. Did you want to check it out?"

Everything seemed fine and the kitchen, in particular, looked amazing. This was another place where upgrades must have been done in the past, though the cabinets looked original.

After they left, Addie walked into the room and started loading dishes into the dishwasher. She looked at me and smiled. "I'll start the dishwasher as soon as you get back with the detergent for it!"

"I can take a hint."

CHAPTER 23

Addie and I worked out a deal and she started working full-time until she got through all the rooms at least once. We'd figure out what to do after that when we got there. I was spending money more quickly than I'd planned, but the sale of my old house was on target so I expected a block of funds to come my way in another month or so. My furniture from Chicago would get here shortly and I didn't want to put it in storage unless I needed to, so I thought I'd put it somewhere in the house.

When I stopped by on Wednesday afternoon, Addie had finished cleaning out the cabinets and was running the last load of dishes through the dishwasher. She had also cleaned out the curio cabinet and washed the china and crystal by hand, then put them back. "So, Lou, I washed the curtains from the kitchen, laundry room and maid's quarters, but what do you want me to do about the drapes in the dining room and living room? I've vacuumed them off but they need to be cleaned."

I looked around. "And we need to do the carpet from the living room. Can we just take them all where you took the dining room carpet?"

"Sure, I can take them down tomorrow and run them over there."

"You know, Addie, you're coming along quite well with the downstairs. Once you get that finished, I'd like you to clean out the storage room up on the third floor. I need to get my furniture stored here until I figure out where I want it."

"That room will be easy to clean up since it's mostly empty. Won't take long at all. Do you want to do the basement too?"

"That is pretty much last on the list, but it has to get done sooner or later. There's a lot of stuff down there that I'll probably just give away or throw out. Oh, by the way, the handyman is coming by tomorrow to replace the windows, lubricate the garage doors, and clean the gutters, so if you find anything else that he needs to do, let him know. There's also a roofer coming over the next day to check out the roof, so don't be surprised to see people with ladders climbing around outside."

"If you want, I can bring up some of the wine bottles from the basement. There's a bunch of them there."

"Yeah, sure, but don't get your hopes up. After this long, most of them probably went bad. Are you a wine drinker?"

"Once in a while."

***

When I walked into the house the following afternoon, I was met by a rolled-up carpet, a pile of drapes and a four-year-old girl. The last one was a surprise, but when she saw me walk in she turned and ran into the kitchen, so I followed her.

Addie turned around as I walked in. "Oh, Lou, I hope you don't mind. My mom couldn't watch Marcie today, so I brought her along with me. She didn't get in the way at all."

While I found that last part a little hard to believe, I ignored it and knelt down in front of the girl, whose arm was wrapped around her mother's leg. "Hi, Marcie. That's a pretty name for a pretty girl. My name is Lou."

This got a big grin and when I held out my hand to shake hers, she glanced at her mother, who nodded, then took her hand out of her mouth and stuck it in mine to shake. Her smile was just like her mother's—warm and open.

Addie chuckled at all of this, especially when I wiped my hand on my shirt. "Her name is Marcelle, but we all call her Marcie."

Turning back to the girl, I said, "Well, Marcie, it's nice to meet you. Did you like it over here at my house today?"

"No, I want my toys."

Well, at least she was honest. "Hmm, we'll have to think about that a little bit."

"When my mommy says that it means no."

"Umm, well, that's interesting," I said as I stood up.

"Lou, I found the bottle of Scotch you brought over. Would you like me to pour you some?"

"Sure, that would be great."

At that, Marcie ran off into the living room and jumped onto the rolled-up rug, then promptly fell down laughing.

As Addie walked back into the room she said, "I'm really sorry. I just didn't have anywhere else to take her."

"I'm not paying double for having two of you here, am I?"

Addie broke out into a laugh. "No sir!"

"Actually, I'm glad you brought her along. She's adorable and has your smile. I see you got a lot more done today, but how did you move the rug?"

"The handyman guy, George, helped me with it; I can take it to the cleaners when I leave today. He worked on the garage and took the measurements for the windows he's replacing. He also asked if you wanted him to paint anything around here, said the front trim needs some touch-ups. He's coming back tomorrow to finish the windows, so if you want him to, I can tell him. Oh, and he said he could help you out with the cars in the garage if you want. He seemed really interested in the old one."

I counted things off on my fingers. "One, the rug can wait until you don't have Marcie, or else I can take it tomorrow, whatever works for you. Two, yes to the touch-up painting on the front trim, if he can match the colors. Three, do you know if he got the garage doors lubricated? Four, did you bring up any of that wine?"

She grinned at me again. "One, I'll get it tomorrow. Two, I'll tell him what you said. Three, yes, he put new batteries in the remotes and lubricated all of the doors and they all work fine now. But I don't know how you're going to move those cars with the flat tires. Four, no, not yet, but I can get some right now if you want."

I raised my glass of Scotch. "I think I'm good for right now, maybe tomorrow. But I was thinking, since you're trying to keep your car out of sight, you can park in the garage if you want. That way Drea won't see it."

She looked down at the floor and pressed her lips together before responding. "I guess we don't have to worry about that anymore."

I raised my eyebrows, waiting.

"Aunt Drea rang the doorbell this afternoon and Marcie let her in."

"Oh... How did that go?"

"She told me I'm an adult and can do whatever stupid things I want to, but I had no business bringing my daughter over here after all of the horrible things that happened."

I wasn't really sure what to say. We'd both known this was coming and it was none of my business. "Addie, do you want to do something different about this?"

She looked at me defiantly. "No! I came here on my own looking for a job and you're very nice to me. I said I would do this, and I want to stick it out."

For a moment I paused. "Did you say anything about Sara?"

"Who's Sara?"

I had forgotten about Marcie. Addie looked over at her. "She's just a friend of Lou's."

Marcie's eyes got wide. "Is she your girlfriend?"

Addie turned away to cover her mouth, hiding a smile. This little girl could melt anyone's heart.

"No, she's not my girlfriend, she's just someone that I know."

"Oh." And she turned and went back into the living room to play.

I kept my voice low. "You might want to keep her away from Drea for a while. If she says something about Sara, you'll hear a lot more than you heard today."

Addie nodded. "You're right, and it would upset Aunt Drea immensely. She loved those kids, especially Sara."

CHAPTER 24

Over the next week, the downstairs got cleaned up and was pretty much fully functional. I thought about moving in but hadn't decided yet since the second floor still needed to be done and my furniture would get here very soon.

On Saturday morning I showed up a little later than usual. I'd stopped by the florist on the way over and also brought Furb with me to let him wander around while I worked on stuff. The door was unlocked so I figured Addie was already there, but when I walked in the front door, I didn't hear her moving around. So I put down the cat and started looking for her.

She was in the kitchen, sitting at the table, sobbing. When I walked in, she jumped up and went to the sink to wash her face. "Sorry, I'll get to work now," and then she started out of the kitchen.

"Addie, come back. Tell me what's wrong. Did Drea come by again?"

She started to tear up again. "No, my sister is getting married."

This was confusing. "You're upset because your sister is getting married?"

"No, you don't understand."

"Please explain it to me. Don't you want her to get married?"

"No, that's all wrong. I'm happy that she's getting married. It's just that I've lived with her for the last several months and now she wants me to move out."

"Ah, I think I see. So what are your plans?"

"I don't know. Apartments are expensive. Even though you are very nice and pay me more than I was making before, it would be a stretch. Without a steady job, no one will rent to me, and besides, I'm not sure how long I'll be working here. I don't know where Marcie and I are going to go."

"Is there room at your mother's place?"

"No, she just has a one-bedroom for herself. Watching Marcie is not a problem but she can't have the two of us living there. Her apartment manager would throw her out if he found us there."

Furb walked into the room. Addie jumped, then realized what she was seeing and settled down. "And who is this?"

"This is Furball, though I just call him Furb most of the time. He's been with me for several years now, since he was a kitten."

She knelt down and put out her hand to him. "Well, he sure is a big cat. I haven't seen one quite this big. Is he a special kind?"

"He's a Maine Coon cat. They get bigger than most. He's probably about full-grown now, though he may get a little heavier as he gets older."

Furb, always the social cat, decided Addie was an all-right person and let her pet him while he purred like a small motorboat.

"I hope you're not allergic to cats. Sorry, I should have asked before I brought him over."

She shook her head. "No, I like them a lot. I even promised Marcie we could get one when we get our own place, but I don't know when that will be, especially now." She wiped some more tears off her face and stood up. "Look, I'm sorry. It's just that my sister caught me by surprise this morning and I'm still trying to figure things out."

I watched her working to regain her composure.

"I'll go ahead and get to work now. Second floor, right?"

"Addie, I have a question for you."

"Yes?"

"Well, the maid's quarters are empty and you have them cleaned up, and there's a new mattress for the bed. What would you think of moving in here for a while?"

Her eyes got big. "Oh, Lou, I couldn't do that. I thought you were planning on moving in there pretty soon."

"I haven't decided yet. So if you want it you can have it."

"But what about Marcie?"

"Well, her too, of course. Is there room for her in there with you?"

She took a deep breath and then threw her arms around my neck. "Oh, thank you! You're so nice to me." And then she started crying again.

I wasn't sure what to think, so I just put my hands on her back and let her cry.

CHAPTER 25

Three days later my furniture from Chicago arrived. The movers were surprised that I wanted everything on the third floor, but fortunately, there wasn't a lot of it, so they started carrying the couch, bed, and other stuff up there.

Of course, that was also the day Addie wanted to move in, which led to some confusion. She had very little other than clothes, but she brought Marcie's bed. Since she still used a toddler-sized bed, it fit into the room along with the double bed that was already there.

With all the excitement planned for the day, I left Furball back at my apartment. He'd adapted to the new house very quickly and loved wandering around looking into all the rooms and closets and under the beds. The only problem was finding him when it was time to leave. On the other hand, he'd found a place on the living room floor that got direct sunlight in the late afternoon, so he was often snoozing there.

The movers had a few questions about how to arrange stuff in the storage room so I could get at things that I might need. After that, I helped Addie bring in stuff from her car while she figured out where to put them. We shifted the bed over to make room for Marcie's. While we did this, Marcie ran around the house, as usual, but she stayed out of the way of the movers like Addie had warned her.

I looked over at Addie after the furniture was where she wanted it. "Is this going to be okay? There's not a lot of room in here and you won't have much privacy."

"It's fine. We shared a room at my sister's place, so we're both used to it. And Marcie's a very sound sleeper, so I don't have to be really quiet. Anyway, I can always go into the kitchen or something if I want to sneak away from her. That's okay, isn't it?"

"Of course, that's fine. You're living here."

She looked like she had a question she wasn't sure she wanted to ask. "Lou, you know how Marcie and Furb were playing when they were both here the other day?"

I hesitated. "Yes?"

"Well, I thought maybe you could just let Furb stay over here. We can take care of him so you don't have to worry about him, and it will be more interesting for him too."

I grinned at her. "Are you trying to kidnap my cat?"

She screwed up her face, knowing that I was joking. "Well, I think it would be catnap… no wait, that doesn't work either, does it?"

"Actually, that sounds like a great idea. Sometimes I leave the television on for him in the apartment, with the sound on low. He likes to watch Animal Planet, but this would be more stimulating for him. Do you plan on keeping Marcie here with you during the day?"

"Oh, no. I'm going to take her over to Mom's just like I have been. She doesn't get into much trouble, but still, I'll get more done if she's not here."

"Well, it's okay if Marcie stays here, too, if you want. That's fine with me. I'll bring Furb over tomorrow along with his food and stuff."

She grinned. "Great, Marcie will love it!"

CHAPTER 26

By Friday things settled back into a groove. I left work in mid-afternoon and got to Rose House a little earlier than normal. This time I was greeted by Marcie and her faithful companion, Furb, so I knelt down and Marcie gave me a big hug while I petted the cat. Both seemed happy.

Hearing noises from the kitchen, I went that way looking for Addie. She was putting away some dishes in the cabinets but looked up when I walked in.

"Hello, Lou."

She seemed far more reserved than I'd expected, which immediately concerned me. But then, I knew she was working on the office and that wasn't a pleasant task.

"How are things going today, Addie?"

"Things are fine. I'm working on the second floor now." Still too quiet.

"Cleaning up the office?"

"Well, is it the office or the den?"

This was a little more like her. "Or the library?" I added.

"Or the library. What do you want to call it?"

"Well, if I use any of those three names, it all means the same room."

She raised an eyebrow. "Can't decide, huh?"

"Probably will sooner or later, but you never know. Is there something wrong up there you want to talk about?"

She shook her head and turned back to the dishes.

I stood there a moment but she ignored me. "Addie, what's wrong? I've never seen you this quiet."

She stopped what she was doing and turned around. "I also cleaned out the conservatory today." Then she stuck her head around the corner. "Marcie, is the door from the conservatory to the garden closed?"

We heard little steps running away, then back. "Yes, Mommy, it is."

"Well then, since it's nice and sunny out there, why don't you and Furb go out there and play for a little while. Just be sure you don't let him outside."

"Okay, Mommy." Then we heard more steps and a door opening and closing.

I stood there waiting. There was something going on.

"Lou, I'm not sure how to put this..." and then she paused.

"Sit down, Addie, and tell me what is wrong. We'll fix it."

We both pulled up chairs and sat, but Addie was quite upset.

She looked down at the table. "Marcie asked me today if she could play with the neighbor girl."

I looked at her, surprised. "I don't know of any young kids around here, but sure, that's fine with me."

She met my eyes and held them. "The one with the flower."

I caught my breath. "She can see Sara?"

"Apparently. I asked her to point her out to me and she waved at a spot in the side yard over close to the Marchants' yard, but I didn't see anything. I asked her to describe her to me, pretending I was playing a game, and she said the girl was bigger than her with yellow hair and lots of curls, and she was carrying around a flower."

I stared at her, dumbstruck.

She continued, "Furb seemed to be looking at exactly the same spot."

"And you saw nothing?"

"No. Kwan was here today pruning the roses and I asked him if he saw anyone. He didn't either."

"Addie, I don't know what to say."

She gave me one of her little grins. "Well, at least you're not crazy."

When I stopped laughing, I got up. "I want some Scotch. Do you want some?"

"I think so."

I poured us both some and sat back down.

"Did Marcie say anything else about Sara?"

"No, not really, just that she saw her in the yard a couple of times this afternoon." She stopped and took a sip of her Scotch, then wrinkled her nose. "I'm not used to this stuff."

"It's an old habit. They say you develop a taste for it. But what do you think we should do about Marcie and Sara?"

"Well, I sure don't want them playing together, but I don't know how to stop her without upsetting her. Today when she asked, I just told her it was time to take a bath and that distracted her, but I don't know what will happen next time." She took a bigger sip of the drink this time, then paused for a moment. "You know, it's annoying sometimes. You see Sara, and Marcie and Furb see her so why can't I? Or Sergeant Johnson?"

"Well, she's a cop. She might be lying to us."

That got a grin that was a little bigger.

"Addie, are you having second thoughts about staying here?"

She looked undecided. "Well, yes and no, but I don't really have anywhere else to go. And I don't want to call it quits... I'm not a quitter. Besides, you plan to move in here, what will you do when you see her?"

"Well, that's a little different. I knew what I was getting into when I bought the house. You didn't and apparently thought I was crazy, not that I blame you."

She smiled again. "You know better than that, but it's just so frustrating and now I'm not sure how it's going to affect Marcie."

"Look, if it would be any better for you, I can be a reference for you and tell whoever that I plan on keeping you working here forever. That should at least help you get an apartment."

She screwed up her mouth. "And lose out on my free rent?"

"It's not a suggestion, just an offer, if that is what you want to do. I'm just trying to help you do what is right for you and your daughter. There are other jobs out there too, if you want to think about that. There's an opening at my insurance office if you're interested. And Marie's has a job opening posted in the window of the flower shop. You could do that and just work here on weekends, or whenever." I paused for a moment, thinking. "Or you can stay here as long as you want. It's up to you."

She took a bigger drink again. "Lou, you've been very nice to me and I'm glad to be here. It's much better than Henry's Fried Chicken where the manager watched me every minute to make sure I wasn't goofing off. Here I get to do things my own way and I like that. And you pay me a lot better than the fast food job. I don't want to leave."

"Fine, like I said I really don't want you to leave, but what about Marcie?"

"Well, I don't know. I guess we'll just see how it goes."

CHAPTER 27

The following day, we checked out the progress in the den-office-library, as Addie started calling it, to determine what exactly to do with it. The floor-to-ceiling shelves lined two walls of the room, each with its own rolling ladder. The shelves were pretty much filled with books from the Dylans and Addie wanted to know what I wanted done with them.

"Well, for now, I think we should clean off each shelf and dust off the books and put them back. But when you take them down, could you flip through each one to make sure there are no loose papers in them? If there are, I'd like to see them, though they will probably get thrown out." I paused. "I'm not sure what I'm looking for."

"Any particular order you want them put back in?"

"Exactly the same order they are in now?"

"You're kidding, right?"

"Unfortunately, no. I don't know why, and it's probably stupid. I'm still trying to piece together some reason why all this happened here, and I don't know where to look. Maybe the sequence of the books will tell me something, maybe not. It's a long shot, I guess."

Addie rolled her eyes at me. "You know that's going to take a long time. I think you're getting a little obsessive about this house."

I smiled. "That and a lot of other things, but remember, I don't want you to run out of things to do!"

She laughed. "I don't think that's likely to happen anytime soon."

We heard the doorbell ring and then little feet running downstairs, so I left Addie to her project and went down to see. Marcie had let Sandi in.

"Hey, Sandi, good to see you."

"I see you have another helper here in the house."

"Sure thing, though this one is a little harder to keep in line than her mom."

She grinned. "I can believe that. Anything exciting going on here?"

"Addie started cleaning out the den— not one of her favorite tasks, but so far it's just slow going, one room at a time." I changed my focus for a moment. "Marcie, why don't you go help your mother upstairs while Sergeant Johnson and I go walk in the garden?"

She put her hands on her hips and looked at me, then left and went to help.

"The first time I met Marcie, a couple of years ago, I thought then she was going to be a handful. That opinion hasn't changed in the least." As we walked outside, Sandi said, "I assume you want to tell me something without them around?"

"Not them, just Marcie. Addie told me something interesting the other day." As we walked a little farther from the house I told her about Marcie wanting to play with the neighbor girl.

She stopped and turned, looking at me, "Please tell me you made this up."

I shook my head. "Ask Addie. I just don't want to make a big deal of it when Marcie can hear me. Knowing her, it would probably make her *more* interested in Sara."

"You haven't told her anything?"

"Addie knows the whole story, of course, but we haven't said a thing to Marcie. How would you go about doing that, anyway? She thinks it's a neighbor girl. And before you ask, I didn't put them up to this."

Sandi rolled her eyes. "This just keeps getting stranger and stranger."

"Oh, by the way, Addie thinks Furball sees her too."

She wrinkled her mouth. "Do you know any pet psychologists?"

"Funny, Sandi."

As we walked back into the house, she commented, "This sure looks a lot better than before. Seems like Addie is doing a great job."

"She is. She takes it very seriously and does things on her own that I would never have thought of."

"Are you planning on putting your furniture in here?"

"The Chicago house was small. Clara and I didn't buy much, nowhere near enough to fill this."

"Have you closed on the house up north already?"

"Should happen next week. I'll be glad to get the check from it; this place has been pretty expensive so far, though I think most of the big things are behind us now."

"And what about the insurance claim for your wife?"

"Well, I have a lawyer working on that one. Sounds like the other driver is likely to do jail time, though he is out right now but without a license. He has a pretty good lawyer on his end, too. He's going to need it."

Johnson nodded as we walked into the den. "Hi, Addie."

"Oh, hi, Sergeant Johnson. What brings you by?"

She put a hand on Marcie's head. "Just making sure Lou's not overworking you two."

Marcie grinned and went back to dusting a book that her mom handed her. At the rate she was going, the library would be clean in about twelve years, but it kept her occupied.

"Addie, it looks like you got the walls cleaned up pretty good."

She looked at her. "There are still some stains that don't want to come out, but the pieces of, um, dirt are gone."

Marcie looked up. "We had dirt on the walls?"

Addie nodded. "Sometimes it happens."

Johnson looked at me again. "You know, you could get some help for her. There are professionals who do this kind of cleanup."

Before I could respond, Addie jumped in. "Don't go giving him ideas. I can do this just fine and I don't need anyone to help me."

Johnson shook her head and we went back downstairs. "Is she worried about being out of a job?"

"Probably, but with them living here now I don't see how that's going to work."

"Seems like you've got yourself in a pickle."

I shrugged. "We'll figure something out."

CHAPTER 28

On Sunday, George the handyman showed up to help me with the cars while Addie continued working upstairs.

"So, George, how do you suggest we go about this?"

"Well, Mr. Navelliere, I brought over some oil and my air compressor and a spare battery, plus a bunch of tools we might need. For cars that have been sitting for a long time, one of my mechanic buddies suggested that we should change oil first to a lighter weight, then squirt some into each cylinder through the spark plug hole and turn the engine over by hand just to make sure it isn't frozen up. If that works okay, then we can replace the plugs and try to start it, but I'll check the hoses and stuff first to make sure they seem all right. You know you'll have to get both of them checked out if we get them running, right?"

"Yeah, I know. New tires, change the fluids, that kind of stuff. But it would be nice to have them running. When you say turn over the engine by hand, you mean with the starter, right?"

"No, I'll just use my wrench to turn it over a few times. That way if the engine is locked up, we'll know right away and won't break something else. So, which one did you want to start with?"

"Which one is more valuable?"

George looked at the two cars. "Well, the SUV is a lot newer, but the Cadillac is a classic and probably worth more."

"Then let's start with the SUV."

George grinned and popped the hood on the Lincoln. "Yeah, I'd do the same thing. Oh, by the way, Addie found keys for both of these in the house, so that should make things a lot simpler once we're a little further along."

"Great, so what do you want me to do? I'm not much of a mechanic."

"Well, just hang around for a while. I'll want some help when we actually try to start them. I'm going to start draining the oil and then pull the plugs while that's going on. Shouldn't take more than a few minutes."

I watched him working, trying to follow the process. He kept up a running conversation while he worked, telling me more than I ever wanted to know about cars. "So after we get done with the cars, are you about through with me for a while here?"

"You have something else lined up?"

"No, just wondered if I should start looking for something."

"Well, the study needs painting once Addie finishes cleaning it up. Knowing her, that will only take a couple of days, so you can do that next."

He grimaced at me. "Addie told me about that room."

"Is that a problem?"

"No, I was on active duty when I was in the service. Saw more of that stuff than I wanted to, but it doesn't bother me. I guess we should put on a coat of primer. You want the wallpaper stripped, right?"

"Yeah, strip it, prime it, paint it."

"I can do that whenever Addie is ready. Anything else?"

"Well, I need to get started cleaning out the basement. There's a lot of stuff in there and most of it will wind up in the trash or go to charity. Some of the stuff is pretty big, so you could help me with that if you want."

"Be happy to."

George finished squirting the oil in the cylinders and was ready to try turning it over. He pulled a socket out of his tool box and put it on a handle, then slowly applied pressure somewhere on the front of the engine block. The bar moved smoothly, so he gave it a few more turns to get the lubrication started. "This is going good so far. I'll get some fresh oil in her and swap batteries, then we'll try to start it."

He was working on that when Addie showed up. "Lou, I'd like to take Marcie over to my aunt's house tomorrow evening, if that's all right with you."

I nodded. "I don't see a problem. You've been working here a lot more than I ever expected you to. You need a break."

She smiled. "Well, there's a birthday party for one of my cousins. We haven't seen them in a couple of months, so it should be fun."

"Yeah, sure. Oh, and George is going to strip the wallpaper and paint once you're done in the study, so just let him know when you're close so he can plan that out."

"Okay. Shouldn't be more than a few days."

She went into the house just as George finished adding oil and putting the plugs in.

"Well, we're ready to try turning her over. I've got a spare battery hooked up, so I guess we'll just see what happens."

I took the key and sat in the driver's seat. It was pretty dusty in there even though the windows had been up. When George gave the ready signal, I turned the key. The engine spun briefly, made a deep whump, then died.

"Turn the key off. I think I'm going to have to get new plugs for it. I can run down to the parts store and be back in about fifteen minutes, then we can try again."

While he did that, I looked around the garage. An old lawn mower in one corner was covered with dirt. Since there was no grass anywhere in the yard, I wasn't sure how old that was. Some old furniture next to it was also filthy. All of it could get thrown out.

I got bored out there and went back into the house, where Addie and Marcie were busy in the den. "Anything I can do to help?"

Addie looked at Marcie, then me. "We've got it under control for now. You might want to look around the master bedroom and let me know if there is anything special you want done there."

I was about to do that when I saw George pulling back into the driveway, so I went back out to the garage.

With the new plugs, the Lincoln started right up, though it was running a little rough.

George grinned at me. "One down, one to go. I'll put air in the tires, then when you want you can take it into the shop."

"Can you get them down there for me? I'm trying not to take too much time off work right now. Just give them my phone number and I'll make the arrangements to get the work done."

"Sure thing. I'll do that tomorrow."

We went through the same process on the Cadillac, but it was even easier. It started right up without a hiccup, so I left George happily working on his projects and went back into the house.

On a whim, I wandered into the basement and turned on all the lights. Lots of dust, junk, and wine. I pulled a couple of bottles from the two wooden wine shelves down there and dusted them off. One red, one white; that worked.

Back upstairs, I rummaged around in the kitchen cabinets until Addie walked in and told me where the corkscrew was stored. Since she was at a temporary stopping point, I grabbed two glasses and opened the bottle of Pinot Grigio. The cork didn't look good, but I took a taste anyway. It tasted like vinegar, so I dumped it out.

Addie stood there watching while I did this. "Would you like me to do that?"

I handed her the corkscrew. "I'm not sure how much of this is going to be any good."

She pulled the cork on the Cabernet Sauvignon and handed it to me.

"You didn't learn that working in a fast food restaurant."

She laughed. "This is the South. Eating is important, and wine is an important part of meals. I think you're underestimating me." She poured some wine into two glasses and handed one to me.

I was pleasantly surprised by this one. It was full and rich, with hints of fruit and an aftertaste that lingered. I looked over at her. "You have the magic touch. And I will try not to underestimate you ever again. I apologize."

She shrugged and sipped her wine.

CHAPTER 29

The next few weeks were hectic. On the one hand, George got both cars fixed, up to date and detailed, so I would have two spare cars to use once I got the licensing done. On the other hand, I had repeated conversations with my lawyer and the insurance company representatives who wanted to get things settled quickly. I have no problem with quickly, but in this case, they meant before I really had time to think about it.

Addie finished cleaning in the study and George then took over there and started the painting project that we'd discussed. I looked over a few loose papers that Addie had found in some of the books, but nothing was very interesting. Then, I also wanted to go through all the paperwork in the desk, much of which seemed related to Harper's business dealings, but I worked on that in the evenings so I wasn't in the way when George was working.

In the meantime, Addie had moved on to cleaning up the boys' bedrooms, then went on to Libby's room and the master bedroom. We left Sara's room for last. The only Sara activity was when Marcie said she saw the 'girl with the flower' in the yard again, but I hadn't seen anything.

That Wednesday I managed to get out of the office early, stopped to buy my rose, and went over to the house. When I got there I saw Addie's car in the garage, but no sign of her or Marcie, who lately just stayed here since Marcie's grandmother had changed shifts at work and now slept during the day. But that was fine with me.

I thought I heard some noises upstairs, so I went on up. No one was in the boys' rooms or the study, but I thought I heard water running. I walked into the master bedroom and noticed the bathroom door was closed, so I knocked. Marcie opened the door to the bathroom and smiled. I looked up and stopped, mouth open and eyes wide. Addie was washing the wall of the shower with her back to me. I watched the water running down her bare back, across her buttocks, and down her legs.

"Hi, Lou." This from Marcie.

Addie must have heard her. "Did you say something, baby?" Then she glanced over her shoulder. She let out a squeak and dropped the sponge. She spun around to face me and then tried to cover herself with her hands. Realizing her mistake, she spun back around and yelled "Go away!"

Marcie, startled, began to cry, so I picked her up and left, closing the door behind us.

A little while later Addie came down into the living room, but I had a hard time telling what kind of a mood she was in. Marcie and I were sitting in the middle of the floor, piling up blocks. After they were eight or nine high, Furb would walk over and swat them with his paw so he could watch them fall. Marcie thought this was hilarious. I agreed.

Since Addie wasn't in a mood to talk, I got up. "I want to look over some of the papers in the study. Let me know if you need anything."

"Would you like me to bring you some Scotch?" She seemed reluctant.

"Sure, that would be great."

The papers were pretty meaningless so I tossed them in a pile for recycling. Then Addie showed up and set my drink on the desk. I looked intently down at the papers, keeping my eyes away from hers. "Addie, I'm sorry about walking in on you before. I had no idea what you were doing until Marcie opened the door. I thought you were still working on the boys' rooms."

She was still cautious, but it seemed like some of the anger was dropping away. "I was, but I thought it would be nice if I got the master bedroom ready for you. I wanted to surprise you. It wasn't your fault, I should have known better."

I paused for a moment, then added, "I appreciate what you were trying to do. It will be nice to get moved in here so I don't have to run back and forth every day. Thanks." Another pause.

She screwed her mouth up again to say something, but then the feeling passed and she shook her head and walked away.

CHAPTER 30

The following day, after a bit of searching, I found Addie in the library.

"Lou, I need to talk to you." As I looked at her, she still seemed upset about the shower incident, not that I blamed her.

"Okay, Addie, about what?"

"What do you want done with the clothes from the bedrooms? I went through the closets in the master and put them all in piles. Are they going to charity?"

"That sounds good. Do you know of one that will come and pick them up?"

"Well, I can take them somewhere, if you like. There are a couple of places in town that clean stuff up and resell it."

"Whatever works best for you is fine. I don't care where they go, but I don't want to just throw them out."

"And... when I started going through the pockets, I found these in one of the suits." She handed me two one-hundred-dollar bills.

"The house is starting to pay for itself!" I put one in my wallet and handed the other to her.

"What do you want me to do with this?"

"It's yours. A bonus. Do what you want with it."

"But it's your money."

"And you do all the work. Do you want to argue about taking it?"

Small smile. "Well, thank you, sir!"

"Oh, Addie, a question for you. The last couple of days, Marcie started calling the cat Oo-ay. Why is she doing that?"

Addie laughed and tried to hide it, covering her mouth. "When we went over to my cousin's house for that birthday party, Marcie started talking to them about Furb. Since our heritage is Acadian, many of us speak French and they were trying to teach some to Marcie, so they asked her where the cat was: '*Où est le chat?*' It sounds the same. I guess she just thought it was a name."

"*Umm, parlez-vous français aussi?*"

"*Mais oui, Monsieur!*"

I grinned. "Sorry, that's about all the French I know."

"Making progress with the papers in the study?"

"Well, today it's the library. I went through most of them and the only thing of any interest was the registration papers for the two cars, so I can take care of getting licenses for them later this week. Oh, did you bring up any more of the wine from the basement?"

"No, do you want some?"

"Not now, but George and I are going to start cleaning out downstairs. How much room do we have for bottles in the kitchen?"

"There's room there for about twenty bottles, but there's a lot more than that downstairs. Do you want them all moved out?"

"Yes. I thought it would be nice to empty the basement out entirely and clean it up as good as possible, then paint the walls white. It will look a little brighter and nicer."

"Really? Most people don't paint their basements."

"You're right, they don't, but it seems like a good idea to get it cleaned up."

"You're the boss."

"Addie, you're leaving Sara's room alone for now, right?"

"Haven't touched it."

"Let's still leave that one for last."

She looked at me, serious. "Do you really think it makes a difference? Do you think she might leave if we change things?"

I pulled out a chair and sat down. "Honestly, I have absolutely no idea. I don't know what makes a difference and what doesn't. Sara just seems to come and go on her own schedule and I don't know why she is here or what she wants or what I can do."

"You could try asking her."

"When I talk to her, it seems like she hears me, but the only response is a tilt of the head, and I'm not even sure that's because I said something."

"I have this feeling you will figure it out one of these days."

"I also found a white rose in Chicago."

Addie hadn't heard about the rose that had showed up right after Clara died, so she listened while I told her the story.

"In Chicago? How does that work?"

I shook my head. "Beats me. I'm shooting in the dark here. I'm not sure what I've gotten into."

"Looks like you're going to need more Scotch!"

I laughed. "You may be right, but I have enough to hold me for now."

CHAPTER 31

A couple of days later I took the day off work to get more stuff done around the house. Addie was still making good progress on cleaning, George started moving stuff from the basement out to the empty garage bay, Kwan fertilized and pruned all the roses and with the weather warming up, the plants were starting to perk up and leaf out. Apparently, I was the biggest holdup.

After spending an hour at the Louisiana Office of Motor Vehicles, I got new registrations and plates for both of the cars. I wasn't sure why I needed three cars for only me, but at least now they were available if I wanted to use them, or maybe sell them.

Addie had the master bedroom all cleaned up and the rug and drapes had just come back from the cleaners, so I decided it was time to move my stuff in. George helped me bring the mattress from the Chicago house down from the third-floor storage room. I left the Rose House furniture the way it was, since it was better quality than mine and, besides, I didn't want to start redecorating quite yet. That too would come in time.

After we got the bed set up, Addie and I decided to get my belongings from the apartment, so she and Marcie and I jumped into the Lincoln and went over to work on that. The clothes, dishes, television, and computer didn't take long to load up. I'd lived out of boxes since I got down here. The apartment I'd rented was furnished, so no furniture or big stuff needed to be moved.

By mid-afternoon, everything was moved to Rose House. I was finally moved in, though with a lot that still needed to get done, and then the whole list of things I was thinking about doing later. But it felt good to be in a place of my own again. Just me and Furball, Addie and Marcie, and the ghost. Hmm.

Putting things away in the closets and drawers didn't take very long. Addie and I worked on that while Marcie watched, asked questions, and played. Furb lay on the bed, observing all of this with interest. When we finished with it, Addie asked what else I wanted her to work on, but it was too late in the day to start something new and I shook my head. Then I went down to help George in the basement while she went back to work a little on the boys' rooms.

George had already taken twelve boxes of unknown stuff from the basement out to the garage, but the bigger things remained. Much of it was dark, heavy furniture that was going to take two people to carry. I looked around the space. It was dusty and dim, though light came from a couple of small windows and four ceiling lights, but I really thought it would look better once we got it cleaned out and the walls painted.

There were several sets of tables and chairs down there, plus a large desk and various bedroom furniture suites. Along the wall near the steps were the two wine racks—just open shelves, but they kept the wine bottles stored on their sides and it was cooler down here than in the rest of the house, so it was a good place to keep them. We carried a couple of big pieces of furniture out to the garage, but then George had to leave.

Rather than waste my time, I started unloading the wine bottles into boxes. The first few went into the kitchen, but that filled up quickly. After that, I carried some up to the storage room on the third floor. By the time the racks were close to empty, I was tired and ready to quit for the day, so I took a shower and ordered Chinese take-out for the three of us to celebrate the new house.

After dinner, Addie took Marcie into the living room to read to her and I went up to the library, to unwind with a glass of Scotch, but the house felt funny. After a small house in Chicago and then a one-bedroom apartment here, this place was huge. I decided to look around the house once before heading to bed.

The hardwood floors chilled my bare feet, but it felt good after a long day of working and carrying wine. As I came down the stairs, I heard noises from the back of the house where Addie and Marcie were doing something, but decided not to bother them. I turned left at the foot of the stairs and walked into the living room. It was a clear night with a full moon, the room was lighted by the windows and I stood there looking out over the rose bushes to the quiet street.

What happened here seven years ago, and more importantly, why? Perhaps that was a question that would never be answered. A light breeze played with the bushes outside and the leaves on the neighbors' trees were moving gently. It was actually a very lovely setting... nice house, nice neighborhood. What goes wrong with a family when it seems like everything is going well?

I looked out the door at the end of the hall that led to the conservatory. Kwan had replaced the dead potted plants, and with the new ones sitting around it looked nice. It seemed like an ideal place to sit and sip a glass of wine on an evening like this. But not tonight, though I couldn't say why I felt that way. I looked around the side yard, scanning the bushes, but saw no sign of Sara, the girl with the rose and the tears.

I went back upstairs, planning to look into the boys' rooms, but Addie wasn't done cleaning them out yet. Instead, I walked into Sara's room to look around, trying to piece things together.

A large bookshelf overflowed with all sorts of chapter books... Newbery Award winners, comedy books and then, of course, books about horses. It was normal reading fare for an eight-year-old girl. I recognized several titles that I'd read many years back. I guess things haven't really changed that much in the last twenty years or so; kids still like to read many of the same things that I had read.

The desk was covered with more books and some papers that looked like schoolwork. Eventually I would go through them, but not tonight.

On the nightstand was another book, probably the one she had been reading at the time she was killed. Or maybe her Mom had been reading it to her. I thought about turning on the lamp, but plenty of light came in through the open drapes, so I left it off. I picked up a large glass paperweight and looked closer. It was from Disney World. Everything was just so normal. Even the toy box at the end of the bed was piled with stuffed animals, including a unicorn sitting on top.

I turned to go.

Sara.

She stood by the door, watching me. I had no idea how long she had been there. She held her rose in her right hand, hanging at her side. Her face showed tears, or at least traces of them. I saw that even in the moonlight.

"Hello, Sara."

She watched, said nothing. Her eyes moved a little, looking around the room, then back at me.

"Sara, how can I help you? Is there something that you want?"

No reaction, but she still watched me.

"Sara, I want you to be happy, but I don't know what to do."

She tilted her head, just a little. Other than that, I saw no reaction, and then she faded away.

CHAPTER 32

George and I started moving furniture out of the basement the next morning when he got there. A number of large pieces remained to be cleared out and then we needed to move the wine racks. After that, he could start working on it.

"So, Lou, what exactly is it that you want me to do with the basement after all of this is out of here?"

"My original plan was just to get all the dirt out and paint the walls, but I'm rethinking that. Do you have access to a paint sprayer?"

"Yeah, my brother is a painter and he has all sorts of equipment like that. I work with him sometimes when he needs extra help, so I've done all that kind of stuff. He'll loan me one. Did you want that for the walls?"

"No. Tell me what you think about this: if we were to blow out all the dirt and cobwebs between the floor joists down here, we can spray the whole ceiling, joists, wires, pipes, and everything. I thought either a very light gray or maybe white. That would lighten the whole space up and make it look a lot cleaner. Think that will work?"

"Well, sure, if you want. Seems like a lot of trouble for a basement if all you do is store stuff down there, but it would look a lot nicer and brighter."

"So we'd want to do the ceilings first, then the walls, right?"

"That would be the best way, sure. Whenever I paint a whole room I like to work from the top down, so the ceilings, then the walls, then I can even do the floor if you want."

"As big as the house is, I don't need any more room for living space. I even tossed around the idea of putting a pool table in the storage room up on the third floor, just for fun, or maybe in the playroom up there."

We moved furniture out to the garage while we carried on this discussion and finished the last of the pieces. The space looked empty but still dingy.

Grabbing a couple of boxes, we loaded the last few wine bottles into them and carried them up to the third floor. With both of us working, it went pretty quickly.

"I can get my air compressor over here this afternoon and get this place blown out. Then I can shop-vac it to get the stuff off the floor."

"Do you have a hazmat suit? I think you might need it."

"I don't need one of those!"

"Seriously, George, when you blow it out, at least wear goggles and a mask. It's going to kick up a ton of dirt. And open the windows down here too to air it out some, but be sure the door to the first floor is closed or you'll be in big trouble with Addie."

"Well, if you want, I guess I can do that."

With the last of the wine moved out, the only things that remained were the two wine racks. We each grabbed a side of the first one, but it didn't budge. It looked heavy since it was made out of solid wood with a wooden plank back, but we should have been able to move it.

"Oh, Lou, look! He's got it bolted to the wall up here. I guess he didn't want it to tip over."

"Well, it would make a huge mess if that happened. I did some searches on some of these wines and they were pretty expensive, so I guess he was being careful."

George ran out to the garage and brought in his tools. He unbolted it in a couple of minutes; only two bolts near the top held it in place. Then, we carried that one out to the garage. Almost there!

The second rack was set up the same way, with just two bolts, so George pulled them out and we grabbed the rack and started moving it. As we started carrying it away, I glanced to my left.

I dropped my end of the rack and turned toward the wall where it had been, and the opening behind it. The light was dim, but I saw fabric and hair.

I backed away from it until I bumped into the staircase wall, my heart pounding wildly. I couldn't look away.

I reached for my phone, my hands shaking so much I almost dropped it. I hit speed dial and stood there waiting, staring, breathing rapidly.

"Johnson here."

My throat was so constricted I could barely speak. "Sandi, we found the boys."

CHAPTER 33

I ran up the stairs two at a time, with George right behind me. Addie was in the kitchen.

"Lou, you're all white."

"Addie, where is Marcie?"

"Are you okay?"

I forced myself to calm down a little. "Addie, take Marcie and get out of this house. Now! The police will be here any minute and I don't want her around for all this."

"My God, what's wrong?"

I glanced around and didn't see Marcie, but I kept my voice low just in case. "The boys."

Addie's eyes widened and she covered her mouth. Then she realized what she needed to do and went looking for her daughter. I heard the door close behind them a moment later.

George was very pale. I grabbed some glasses and poured us some Scotch, hands shaking. "Here, try this." I chugged mine. Maybe it would calm me a little.

The sirens were dim but approaching quickly and we went to the front door just as two police cars pulled up. Sandi jumped out of the first one and ran to the door. "Where?"

"The basement, behind the wine racks that were bolted to the wall." I grabbed a flashlight out of the drawer and handed it to her.

"Are you sure?"

"All I know is there's at least one body in there. There's clothing and hair. I'm not sure what else I saw."

"Did you touch anything?"

"No, we were moving the wine rack out to the garage when I saw it. We didn't go near it at all."

"Good." She motioned to the other two officers who were with her and they all went down into the basement, Sandi leading.

I pulled out a chair and sat down at the kitchen table, taking deep breaths, trying to regain my composure. George sat down across from me, still looking white and scared. "You think that was the boys that were missing?"

"I think so. Not sure who else it would be. I couldn't tell if that was a body in there or not, or more than one. Honestly, I didn't want to look too close."

He took another swallow of his drink and almost choked on this one. "Yeah, me either. I knew the story of the house, but I never thought we'd run into anything like this."

I heard the side door open and went to look. Addie had come back but without her daughter.

"Where is Marcie?"

She looked as shaken up as we were, but it seemed she wanted to be here. "I left her with Drea. Mrs. Marchant said she was welcome to stay there all day if we needed her to and to let them know what they could do to help."

"How much did you tell her?"

"I just told her and Drea that you found the boys. Marcie was in another room at the time, so she didn't hear it. Both of them were shocked."

"So were we."

George nodded.

"Addie, Sandi is downstairs now with two other officers, but I suspect there will be more of them showing up shortly. I have no idea how long this might take, but I would guess it will be hours."

"Can we have them use the basement door?" She stopped, embarrassed. "I'm sorry, I'm not thinking real clearly right now."

"That's actually a good idea for getting in and out, but there will be lots more questions as the day goes on."

As if on cue, Sandi came up and grabbed a chair. "How much do you want to know?"

"Just give us basics for now. I don't need details."

"Good, because I don't have any details or anything concrete right now. Behind the wine rack is a hole about four feet high and two and a half feet wide. Not sure how deep, maybe a foot and a half, the thickness of the foundation wall. That section of the wall was removed. It appears there are two bodies in the hole from what we could tell. I've got help coming in to go over the scene for evidence. Based on sizes and clothing, my guess is that it's the missing boys, though we won't know for sure until we run tests. From what it looked like, one of them had a crushed skull."

I shuddered and looked over at Addie. By the shaking of her hands, she wasn't handling this very well. I offered my glass to her and she took a sip, then shook her head with distaste, but at least it brought some color back to her face.

Sandi looked at me. "We'll have lots of questions for you later, but what on earth led you to move those wine racks?"

"I wanted to get the basement cleaned up, paint the walls, get rid of all the old junk from the Dylans. George and I moved everything else out, but we wanted to take the wine racks down so he could get to the walls to blow them off and paint. The wine racks were the last thing to do, but they were bolted to the walls. I thought that was just a precaution so they didn't fall over and break all the bottles. Now I'm not sure what to think."

We heard more cars pulling up and Sandi went to meet them. "Is it all right if we just come in through the basement door?" she asked, winking at Addie.

She blushed. "I'm sorry!"

"No, really, it's a good idea. Are you three planning to stay around for a while?" She paused. "Where's Marcie?"

"I took her over next door. She's spending the day with Drea and Mrs. Marchant."

"Okay, good." Then she continued heading out the front door. She paused again, "And the cat?"

I shook my head. "I haven't seen him for a while, but with all the commotion he's probably hiding under a bed somewhere."

"I'll close the basement door so he doesn't come help us investigate."

CHAPTER 34

The next few hours dragged on very slowly. Police were coming and going the whole time, while Sandi pretty much stayed in the basement to oversee the work they were doing.

She did, however, send up a couple of officers to take our statements. There wasn't much for us to say; we went over the details of how we found the opening, why we were moving the wine racks. We answered each of the questions at least a dozen times from different people.

Sandi came up about an hour after we finished the statements. "You guys doing all right? Do you need anything?"

"Not really, just wondering what is going on and how long this might take."

"Well, since all three of you have given us statements, there is no need for you to stay here, from our perspective, but we'd like you to avoid the basement until we're done. Your other question is harder to answer. We won't be done today. There are other things we want to look into before we close this part of the investigation. While I hope we'll complete this tomorrow, right now I can't even say that for sure. If you want, we can put you up in a hotel tonight and we'll leave an officer downstairs tonight. That's your call."

George looked up. "Well, if you don't need me around anymore, then I'll go ahead and leave. Lou, is there anything you want me to do before I go?"

"Not really. I'll close up the garage in a little while. George, it's looking like you get tomorrow off, too."

"That's fine with me." And he headed out to his car.

I looked over at Addie. "What do you want to do for you and Marcie?"

She met my eyes. "Are you planning to stay here?"

"I thought I would. Somebody needs to see if this brings out any ghosts."

She wrinkled her nose at me. "Well, I guess we can stay here too. That way she can sleep in her normal bed."

"She's going to have questions."

"I'll figure out something to tell her." She paused, thinking. "Yeah, I want to stay here tonight."

Sandi looked at her. "You just want to make sure we don't mess up your kitchen, don't you?"

"And the bathroom!"

"I'll talk to whoever is staying here. They'll check on the outside of the house once in a while, but other than that I'll tell them to stick to the basement, kitchen and bathroom so they don't disturb you."

I looked over at Sandi. "You going to say anything about Sara?"

She chuckled. "No, I don't want to lose my job right now, so I think I'll leave that part out. But I'll also make sure to ask in the morning if they noticed anything at all out of the ordinary."

"Then you're done with us for now?"

"Yep. You can go if you want." She grinned, "Just don't leave town."

"Addie, why don't we get Marcie and go out someplace for a nice dinner. I could use a change of scenery."

Addie looked tired. "I could use that too."

As we walked out of the house, the coroner's van was pulling in. It was definitely time to leave.

CHAPTER 35

The police finished the following afternoon, though Sandi asked that we stay out of the basement for a few days until they had everything processed. That way, if there were more questions, they could come back. I didn't see an issue with this, other than that it slowed down part of the progress, so I called George and told him to take a week off. That worked out well for him since his brother planned to start a big painting job and wanted his help.

Things stayed quiet for a few days, though Kwan was a little spooked when he found out the police had been here, and why. Still, he went about his business in the yard. Well, the back part of the yard farthest away from the house, anyway. Sandi stayed in touch, too, but without telling us anything. She remained very professional about this, but we felt frustrated not knowing what they had found. On the other hand, seven years had passed since all this happened, so a few more days didn't really mean much. Addie and I tried to keep from speculating, but that was hard to do.

Drea came by several times and took Marcie over to the Marchants' house with her. Reeve and Lorraine were very nice about the whole thing, but I kept thinking that Reeve must be worried that this would dredge up the whole incident all over again and we would both wind up dealing with a bunch of kooks.

The following Friday afternoon, Sandi called me at work and asked if I would be home later. Since Friday afternoons were pretty quiet in the office anyway, I left early, went to Marie's for a rose, and headed to Rose House.

Addie was cleaning Libby's room while Marcie spent most days visiting with Drea. We'd called a halt to cleaning the boys' rooms when we'd found the bodies even though Sandi hadn't requested it, and I still wanted Addie to leave Sara's room for last, though at this point I doubted that it made any difference.

Sandi showed up a few minutes after I did and the three of us settled into the kitchen to talk. I specifically wanted Addie there since she lived in the house too and was going to have to explain this somehow to her daughter. Plus, she had a right to know; this involved her as much as me, and she'd had the courage to come looking for a job when most people avoided the house entirely.

"Let me go over things once, in detail, and then you can ask questions. I'll answer what I can. Since this case is officially closed and nothing has changed about who we think committed the crimes, I don't have to be particularly careful about what I say.

"First, there were two bodies in the hole you discovered. DNA tests confirmed that those were the two missing boys, just as you suspected. I spent a lot of time going over things with the coroner. Based on blood spatters on the wall edges and the wood walls, it looks like they were both killed in the hole. It's not clear if they were conscious at the time or not, but I would guess not else they would have tried to run. Traces of sedatives were found in both of them, and in both cases, the cause of death was a blow to the head. We also found a baseball bat with blood that matched both boys.

"The hole itself seems to have been put there much earlier. We saw no evidence of recent digging, by which I mean seven years ago, and the house stood untouched until you moved in. I'm not sure how much you saw, but it had plywood walls and floor and also two-by-fours to keep it from caving in. It appears that it was originally intended for storing valuables and we found some things of interest that I'll get to in a minute.

"I'm still trying to piece together a time-line of who was killed when, but we may never know. I guess that Stella was killed first because she might have been able to stop Harper. Past that, it's not clear. I think it was Stella, then the two girls and then the boys, which might have worked out if they were asleep, but the reality is we can't tell. He might have moved the wine rack earlier or he might have just emptied it and swung out one end so he had access.

"I will say that I'm surprised we didn't pick up on this when we went through the house originally. I would have thought someone might have noticed that the wine rack was moved, but none of us did, and I remember looking at them closely.

"In addition to the bodies and the baseball bat, we found a couple of other items in there. There was a small metal storage box on the floor, but it was locked. When we opened it, we found forty-two Saint-Gaudens $20 gold coins, the ones called Double Eagles, from various years. Those were part of the house when you bought it, so they will go to you, but give us a few weeks. Their approximate value is $1,000 per coin.

"A second box in there contained jewelry—rings, necklaces, pendants. To me, they look like diamonds and some of them are fairly large. You'll want to get appraisals on those. When we talked to the Marchants years ago, they mentioned that Stella often wore fancy jewelry, so we were surprised when we didn't find any. At first, we checked bank accounts and finances, but they did not seem to be hurting for money. We thought they might have sold the jewelry for that.

"Another box contained some papers, which we looked at closely. They just seem to relate only to Harper's business dealings and not the murders.

"The one thing that confuses me is why he even put the boys in there. He left Stella lying on the floor, and the girls were in their beds, so why hide the bodies of the two boys? It doesn't make sense to me, but then something obviously set Harper off to trigger all this. Who knows what he was thinking?"

She paused and looked at us. I glanced over at Addie, who had turned white again. I felt a little shaky myself. "Then you didn't find anything that points to a cause?"

She shook her head. "I figured you would ask that. No, we're no closer now than we were seven years ago."

I jumped when the doorbell rang, but Addie got up to answer it. I heard a brief discussion in the foyer, then she walked in with Reeve. He pulled up a chair. Without my saying anything, Addie poured us four glasses of Scotch.

"Sorry to interrupt, but I saw the police car out front and wondered if something else was up."

We sipped our drinks while Sandi brought him up to speed. Of the four of us there, only Sandi had been affected by this whole thing more than Reeve.

Sandi looked over at him. "Reeve, do you have any other ideas about the reasons behind all this? You, Lorraine and Drea are the only ones that really knew the family very well."

"I think saying I knew them well was a stretch. As we talked about originally, Harper was an odd bird, very strict with his kids and wife, and he mostly kept to himself. They came over for dinner a few times, and we were over here once or twice, but you wouldn't call us close friends. Harper kept personal matters close to his vest. Drea told you the same thing. But no one ever saw this coming. It was totally out of the blue."

Sandi persisted. "Any guesses why he hid the bodies of the boys but not the others?"

"Sorry, nothing. I can't even imagine anything that would lead a man to kill his wife and four children."

Addie broke the ensuing silence. "Mr. Marchant, is Marcie okay? I can bring her over here if she's being difficult."

He smiled at her. "Don't you worry. She's just the sweetest little thing we've had in the house in years. Makes me hope my kids start giving us some grand-kids to spoil pretty soon. I'm happy we can help out." He looked over at me. "You know, Lou, I'm sorry you got stuck with finding this, but I am glad the boys were found. That always bothered me. Now if you'll excuse me, I want to go back home and play with a certain little four-year-old."

After he left, Sandi looked at both of us. "I know you want more information. So do I. But we may never get it." She looked at me. "At least you had some idea what you were getting into. Oh, and we finished in the basement. You can seal up the hole or fill it in or do whatever. But if you come across anything strange, let me know, will you?"

CHAPTER 36

When George returned on Monday morning, we discussed the best way to deal with the hole in the wall. After going back and forth with ideas for a while, we decided the best approach was to pull the plywood out, fasten rebar into the floor and walls and then pour concrete to fill it. It probably wasn't a perfect solution, but it would seal it up. Of course, that meant there would be an open hole into the basement, but only for a short while. George got to work on digging in from the outside so we could get started with the concrete.

Addie continued working on Libby's room, which I called the nursery for lack of a better choice. I tried to get away from using the kids' names to refer to the rooms. This was partially to distance myself from what had happened here before. I didn't want to be calling it Libby's room ten years from now. Maybe I was getting a little superstitious, too. This was something new to me, but then so was the ghost. Sara's room, at least for now, we still called Sara's room. I would deal with that sometime.

I put the box of coins and the box of jewelry into the Lincoln. Sandi had left me names and addresses of places that could appraise them. I'd also taken pictures of the contents after Sandi dropped the boxes off, for my own peace of mind. Sometimes I'm a little paranoid.

The coin dealer examined the Double Eagles carefully and confirmed what Sandi had said, though he quoted the value of them slightly higher. No surprises there.

The jeweler, Mister Ortiz, was an older gentleman who had been in the same location for many years. He was pleasant enough when I told him what I wanted and mentioned that Sandi had referred me to him.

When I opened the box, he was taken aback. He didn't say anything for a few moments as he tried to piece things together.

"I recognize most of these pieces here. Sold them to Harper Dylan years ago for his wife Stella. I wasn't doing a lot of high-end business at the time, so they made an impression on me. Harper would come in and tell me what he was looking for and I would either find it or make it. I probably still have the original sales records for them. You must be the one who bought Rose House."

We talked a little while about what had happened lately while he looked through his records. By now everyone in town had heard stories and speculated on the bodies.

"Must have been pretty hard on you, finding the boys like that."

"Yeah. Never thought I'd have to deal with something so shocking."

"We all wondered what happened to them. A lot of us hoped that they somehow got away and were still safe somewhere. They were good kids. Harper brought them in a few times when he picked something up. They were always polite and well behaved. It's a shame about that whole thing. A lot of us would like to forget it ever happened."

"I can see that. I knew the history when I bought the house, but I never expected to find anything like this."

"Well, at least the mystery is cleared up. I hope they rest in peace. Are they burying the boys with the rest of the family?"

"You know, that's a good question. Sergeant Johnson didn't say anything about it. I would assume so, but I'll ask the next time I talk to her."

"Let me know what you find out. I think I'd like to go to the burial, out of respect."

He found the receipts and made copies of them for me. "I expect the current value is right around what I sold these for. Prices haven't changed a lot lately. There is a pair of diamond and ruby earrings that I don't recognize, but other than that everything is accounted for."

My curiosity got the better of me. "Were there any other pieces that you sold them that aren't here?"

He smiled. "Well, normally I wouldn't answer that, but with all of them dead I guess it doesn't matter anymore. I sold him everything in this box plus a couple of watches, but they weren't expensive and wouldn't be worth anything today anyway."

I thanked him and promised to let him know about the burial, then I went to the bank to get a safe deposit box for the stuff. I wasn't sure what I planned to do with it, but I wasn't about to store it in the house.

CHAPTER 37

It rained the day they buried the boys. I didn't expect to know many of the people who might come, but making an appearance was the least I could do, if only in memory of the kids.

The rest of the Dylan family was buried in a vault in one of the older cemeteries in town. It was a small vault, but there was enough room for the six of them. It surprised me how ornate it was, but maybe that said something about Harper.

The other surprise was how many people showed up for the ceremony. Addie and I both went since we felt some kind of kinship with them, or maybe that was the wrong word. Marcie stayed with Addie's mother. The Marchants were there along with Drea. She was the one most upset at this whole turn of events, but then she'd helped raise the boys and had been quite attached to all of the kids. Sandi was there, as I expected, and so was Mister Ortiz, the jeweler I'd talked to. Then I counted about forty other people who were complete strangers to me. I assumed they were friends of the family, but some of them were probably there because of all the scandal associated with the burial.

One of the local priests, Father Clarence, introduced himself to the gathering before he performed the service. He was from the Catholic church the Dylans belonged to and remembered the family and all of the events around them. In his fifties, by my guess, he said some nice things about them and apparently knew the kids from the Catholic school, but he kept the service short. Since no family members were present, most people left right after the service, though a few stuck around, looking like they wanted to say something. A few of these decided to talk to the priest.

I hadn't expected the service for the boys to affect me, but it was so sad that their lives had been cut short because of the parents, or probably just the father. The service also brought back my Catholic upbringing and schooling in New Orleans all over again, though I'd parted ways with it lately.

Sandi, Addie, and I were talking when the priest came over to join us after the others had left. "I'm glad to see so many people showed up after all this time." He extended his hand to me. "I'm Father Clarence. I remember seeing the Dylans in church on Sundays before all this happened. Everyone in town was shocked by the tragedy. Honestly, I would have never suspected Harper was capable of such things, but then I guess you never do expect something like that..."

"I'm kind of an outsider to this whole episode. I knew the background when I bought the house, but I'll admit I got a lot more than I expected."

"I read about that in the papers, and Sergeant Johnson also talked to me last week about finding the boys. I'm sure that was a shock."

"Very much so. I hope I never have to go through something like that again. I suppose it's a lot harder for the people that actually knew them."

"True. While I can't say they were a popular family, they were well-known, mostly from Harper's business dealings. And, with four kids, you tend to know a lot of people. They were good kids, too. But if there is anything I can ever do for you, please come talk to me. I'll be happy to help."

I paused for a moment, deciding. "Father, what do you know about ghosts?"

He looked at me for a long time. "I see you're not kidding as I originally hoped. I have no experience with spirits, but I could discuss it with you. Maybe if we set up something next week, will that work for you?"

We agreed to talk in a few days. I wasn't sure why I'd asked, but if he didn't know about them, who would?

CHAPTER 38

The following Wednesday evening Father Clarence came by after dinner. After introducing her daughter to the priest, Addie took Marcie over to stay with Drea for a little while so we could talk freely, then came back to join us.

I went over most of the details with him about seeing Sara, and that Marcie also saw her, though she thought she was real. He listened carefully to everything I said and tried to take it in without judgment, though he seemed to find that difficult. At least he willingly listened.

"So how many times have you seen Sara?" he asked.

"Probably five or six over the last few months. In various places around the property, both inside and out, and at various times of day ranging from morning to late evening. There doesn't seem to be any pattern to when she shows up, or why."

He turned to Addie. "Have you seen her at all?"

"No. I've been there when Lou saw her, but I didn't see anything. Even Marcie has seen her."

"Tell me about that."

She continued, "We never told Marcie anything about Sara or ghosts or what happened in this house. I thought it might upset her and I didn't want to put ideas in her head. But one day she came to me and asked if she could play with the girl in the garden, the one with the flower. I didn't see anything, so I asked her to describe the girl. She just pointed and said, 'That one.'

"I tried to turn it into a game and asked her for details about the girl. Marcie said she had curly yellow hair and carried a flower. When I asked what she wore, Marcie just said a pretty white dress. I didn't want to push it past that, but when she looked back again, she said the girl was gone."

Father Clarence nodded to himself, thinking this over. "Well, this is certainly interesting. Sara can be seen by some people but not others. Hmm. But she always appears somewhere on this property."

I paused, not sure I wanted to bring this up. "Well, kind of." Then I proceeded to tell him about the rose that had showed up on Clara's stomach in the hospital.

"In which hospital?"

"It was in Chicago."

He stared at me for a moment. "Are you sure that wasn't just some kind of joke?"

"I hadn't said anything about Sara to my friends in Chicago. Enough happened up there with my wife in the hospital and then dealing with her funeral. In fact, I don't think I'd even said *anything* about this house."

He looked confused. "According to contemporary literature, ghosts are typically stuck near the location where they died. Of course, the Church doesn't agree at all with that, but I will admit to a weakness for ghost stories.

"But for her to get to Chicago, and take a rose with her... Well, I've never heard anything like that before. It would mean she isn't tied to the house, but to you. Have you ever communicated with her?"

"I talk to her every time I see her, but it's not clear if she hears me or not. Sometimes I think she does, but I can't really tell for sure."

"Mr. Navelliere, I don't know what to say to you. While I don't doubt what you are telling me, it either seems like an elaborate and very sick prank, or this is something that the Church insists cannot happen. I'd be happy to do what I can, maybe bless the house, sprinkle holy water if you think that might help, but that's about all I can do. Do you think that would put the ghost to rest?"

"No, not really. I think she is here for a reason, but I have no idea what. I know if she were my daughter, I'd hope she got some closure, so I don't want to try to make her go away until she gets what she is looking for. If that is even possible."

He rose to leave. "Well, I'll think about this a little more and do some research. If you change your mind about having the house blessed, let me know. I'm happy to help."

As we walked to the door, I thanked him for coming by and being patient.

Addie looked at me after he left. "What do you think?"

I shook my head. "Unfortunately, that went pretty much as I expected."

CHAPTER 39

"Marcie doesn't like Sara."

I'd just walked into the house after a difficult day at work and found Addie sitting at the kitchen table, looking thoughtful. I looked around. "Where is Marcie?"

"Oh, I took her over to Drea about an hour ago. I should probably go get her... don't want to wear out her welcome over there. But I thought I should talk to you first."

"So, what happened?"

"Well, I finished up the boys' rooms upstairs and she was up there playing, but she got bored and wanted to go outside. Normally I would have said no, but Kwan was out there trimming some of the roses so I figured she would be all right without me watching her. He said he would keep an eye on her just in case.

"I went back upstairs and started cleaning again, but a little while later I heard a door close so I came down to check. She stood by the kitchen door, crying, so I asked why. She said she wasn't hurt, but that the girl in the yard wouldn't even talk to her, she just looked and wouldn't say anything. Apparently, Marcie saw her over by the driveway and went over to talk to her, but Sara didn't respond at all and when Kwan called to Marcie she turned around. When she turned back Sara was gone.

"She wasn't surprised that Sara could disappear that fast, fortunately. But she was upset because she wanted someone to play with. I can't say I blame her for that. After all, I'm not much of a playmate when I clean house. So she started crying, saying the girl was mean. I didn't know what to say. I asked Kwan and he said she was over by the driveway by herself, then she turned around and went into the house. Lou, I'm not sure what to tell her."

I pulled up a chair and sat down next to her. "Addie, you've been working seven days a week lately. I never expected you to do that. Marcie's more important. And the house will wait."

"But you're so good to us, letting us live here for free, and I know you want to get it all cleaned up, but it's taking longer than I expected and I'm afraid you'll get mad at me if I don't get it done soon."

"Whoa, back up. When I offered to let you live here, I didn't expect you to work more days and more hours because of it. It makes it more convenient for you, yes, but it's also nicer for me and Furb to have the two of you around. You've made great progress on the house and got far more done than I expected in the short time you've been here. The house was a disaster and you have the whole downstairs done, plus the master bedroom, which saves me the money for the apartment and the time I spent going back and forth. You are way ahead of my original idea. I thought it might easily take four to five months. So stop worrying about that and spend some time with your daughter. Why don't you start taking a couple of days a week off so she has something else to think about?"

"You're being too nice again."

"No, I'm just concerned about both of you."

She gave me her funny grin. "You always know what to say to get me out of a funk."

"What are you going to tell Marcie about Sara?"

The doorbell rang before she could answer and I heard her talking to Drea, so I went into the foyer.

"Where's Marcie?"

Drea looked over at me, "She's with Mrs. Marchant. They are playing a game for a few minutes so I could come talk to Addie."

Addie chimed in, "Well, you should probably talk to both of us. I think Lou knows more about this than I do."

Drea looked at me suspiciously. "I haven't seen any kids around here lately, but Marcie rambled on about some girl that wouldn't talk to her." She paused, waiting.

"Drea, let's go into the kitchen and sit down. There are some things you need to know."

Addie got me some Scotch, then came and joined us at the table.

I wasn't sure where to start. Maybe the beginning. "Drea, when I found this house I knew nothing about what happened here. I walked by and it surprised me to see such a nice house so obviously neglected. That was the first time I saw Sara."

Her eyes got wide and her face paled. "Sara?"

I nodded. "Before I knew the story, Sergeant Johnson showed me a picture of the Dylans. The girl I saw in the garden was definitely Sara. She stood over by one of the benches. I turned away for just a moment, but when I turned back she was gone."

Drea stared at me, then crossed herself. "Like a ghost?"

"Exactly. When I talked to Sandi about this, she thought I was crazy. She may still think that. But I know what I saw and I've seen her several times since then. She is always wearing the same white dress and she is always carrying a rose with her. Sometimes she is crying, sometimes not, but even then I see the tear marks on her face.

"I've tried talking to her, but she doesn't respond. I don't know if she can. For quite a while I thought I was the only one, but apparently Marcie and Furb see her too."

Drea looked over at Addie. "You should have gotten your daughter out of here the minute you found out about the ghost!"

Addie looked around for a moment, then met her eyes. "Well, actually, I knew about it before I started here."

"Good God, girl, have you lost your senses? Working in a haunted house? Living here, even? I suppose you see Sara too?"

Addie shook her head. "No, I've been with Lou when he saw her, but I didn't. I've never seen her. I got surprised and upset when I realized who Marcie was talking about a couple of weeks ago, but by then we were already moved in. I thought about leaving, finding another job. Lou offered some suggestions. But Sara never tried to hurt anyone. And I'm not a quitter."

Drea started crying. "That poor girl, she wouldn't hurt a soul. She was just the sweetest thing, like little Marcie."

Addie handed her a tissue, waiting for her to calm down.

I put my hand on top of Drea's to reassure her a little. "Drea, I know this is hard to take, but it is part of the reason I bought the house. Do you have any idea why Sara would be hanging around, or why she is always crying?"

After a few more sobs she shook her head. "I don't know, Lou. I just miss her so much. She was my favorite. That poor, sweet little girl."

I leaned back in my chair and took another sip of my drink. "Drea, I'm sorry. I knew this would upset you when you found out. At first I thought I was just seeing things... kind of. It made no sense. But since I was the only one who saw her, I kept it to myself, especially around people who knew Sara."

She wiped the last of her tears away. "Well, I don't know what to think." Turning to Addie, she added, "But you and your daughter should get out of here fast."

Addie looked at her with a firm face. "I need the job, I need a place to stay, and Lou is very nice to me. We're not leaving until I've cleaned up this house like I said I would."

Drea shook her head. "You always were stubborn. Sometimes I felt sorry for your mother even when you were only Marcie's age. I guess you haven't changed much!"

It was all I could do to stifle a laugh, but I said nothing.

Drea stood up, shaking her head. "As soon as Mrs. Marchant and Marcie finish their game, I'll bring her back over." She paused and looked at Addie. "Let me know if there is anything I can do to help you."

CHAPTER 40

"So what are you planning to tell Marcie?"

Addie looked at me and shook her head. "I don't know what to tell her. I'm afraid it will scare her if I tell her the truth. And besides, I don't want her going around talking about the ghost in the house."

"Well, I'm not sure what to tell you. I don't know what I would do in your situation."

I'd told Addie about Clara a while back, but she still surprised me with what she said next.

"What would you have told your daughter?"

I paused for a long time.

"I'm sorry, I shouldn't have brought that up."

"No, it's okay. It caught me off guard and I was trying to figure out the answer. I guess I would have told her as much of the truth as I could... that Sara is a ghost and I don't know why she is here or why we see her, but she has never tried to hurt anyone."

All of a sudden, Addie caught her breath and turned white, staring over my shoulder. I looked.

Quietly, I said, "Hello, Sara. I guess Addie can see you now too."

She said nothing, though I noticed she was crying this time and was rubbing a white rosebud against her cheek, something I'd seen her do before.

"Sara, I wish you could tell us what you need. I know there is a reason you're here, but I don't know what it is. Please believe me, I would do anything I can to help you."

She looked from me to Addie and back. At least her tears stopped for the time being.

Addie, with a shaky voice, asked her, "Sara, why can I see you now when I couldn't before? What can we do to help you?"

Again, I saw no response.

Addie added, "Drea really misses you."

At that, Sara started crying harder. Then a few moments later she disappeared.

I looked over at Addie who was still white and shaking. Softly, I said, "Welcome to the club."

"She was such a beautiful girl. Drea was right. And I can't imagine she would ever hurt anyone."

"No, I don't think she will. But I'm not sure why I think that."

"But she's real, too, isn't she?"

"I guess she is, but in a different way." I passed my drink over to her and she took a sip. "Does this help you at all with what to tell Marcie?"

I said nothing while she thought about that for a few moments.

"Actually, I think it does. Sara isn't a threat to us, she just needs something from us."

Puzzled, I asked, "And you know this how?"

"Call it a mother's intuition."

I shrugged and nodded slowly. "I can't argue with that."

CHAPTER 41

It was a relief when things started getting back to normal. George and some of his friends got the basement wall sealed up, which took several days, and then they needed to wait for the concrete to dry before they pulled off the plywood that held it. While he waited for that, he blew out all of the dust and cobwebs from the floor joists to get it ready for painting, then brought in a power washer and cleaned off the walls and floor. After he finished that, Addie helped out by washing the windows inside and out so the light was better.

In the meantime, Addie had finished the boys' rooms and the nursery, which left me with a problem.

"What's next, Lou, the third floor or Sara's room?"

I thought about that for quite a while. Apparently finding the boys' bodies was not what Sara had been waiting for. Was it something in her room that she wanted me to find? Since I had no way to know, I opted for the third floor. Addie had already cleaned out the storage area up there before I'd filled it up with my stuff, and now only a few rooms remained to be done: the one bathroom, two spare bedrooms, and the playroom. So I told her and she just said "Fine" and went on her way.

A little over a week later, George pulled the plywood off the wall and brought in his paint sprayer. He taped clear plastic over the windows and the door leading into the kitchen so the paint wouldn't get all over them, then he put on his mask and started painting. I looked in through the window while he was working, but so much paint spray was floating in the air I couldn't even see George. At least I heard him moving around, so I figured he was okay.

Reeve stopped by every day or two to see what was going on and how much progress we were making. I should say *they,* since Addie and George did all the work while I just made decisions. But Reeve threw in comments once in a while about the history of the house. I found out they had owned the house next door for over thirty years now, so they'd known all of the Dylan kids from when they were babies. Besides, I think he liked my Scotch, which was fine with me. New town, new neighbors.

After the basement had aired out for a few days, and George had swept the floor again, he took me down there to check out how it looked. "You know, Lou, I would have never thought of doing this, but it sure made a big difference. Everything looks nice and clean and it's a lot brighter down here, just like you said. It might be nice to paint the floor, too. What do you think?"

"I was thinking the same thing."

He gave me a funny look, then shrugged. "You want me to use regular concrete floor paint on it, or should I go with one of the epoxies that they make for garage floors?"

"Let's go with the epoxy. That should last longer. I don't plan on doing this again anytime soon."

"You want the kind with the speckles that get sprinkled in?"

"Sure, a nice medium gray with speckles."

"All right, you got it. I'll get the stuff tomorrow and get started on it. Shouldn't take very long. Once we get that done and we give it a few extra days to dry, you want all of the stuff we moved out to go back in here?"

"Nope, the only things going back in are the wine racks and then the wine. The rest of the stuff I'll donate to charity. Is there anything there you would like?"

"Hmm, not sure. I'll look it over tomorrow and let you know."

As I walked back up into the kitchen, I found Addie waiting for me. "Well, what's next on the list? The third floor is just about finished and that only leaves Sara's room."

"Then, I guess Sara's room it is. But I have a question for you. I thought I'd replace all of the drapes sooner or later, and I know they were pretty dusty so we had them cleaned, but what kind of shape are they in? Will they hold up a few more years?"

"Oh, they're in good shape. I'd guess they were replaced shortly before everything happened, and they're good quality, so they should be fine for a while. I wouldn't worry about that." She paused. "But, you know, I'm going to miss this house."

I thought about it for a while. "Addie, it's really nice for me having you around, and I'll need someone to clean it anyway. Would you consider staying on a permanent basis?"

Her smile lit up the whole room. "Why I'd be happy to, Lou!"

CHAPTER 42

George didn't want any of the furniture in the garage. I wasn't surprised, since a lot of it was an older style which looked fine to me, but wasn't in good shape. Too much wear and tear on it, I guessed. Addie called around and found a home for abused women and children that said they would love to take it. A truck came by the next day and took almost all of it.

The garage was still partially filled with some miscellaneous junk. I didn't know what some of it even was, but then I was never handy or mechanical. I could handle a paint roller, but that was about it. George, however, explained to me in detail what each thing was and why someone would want one, so I put him in charge of getting rid of it. He took a few things, and I told him if he could sell the rest, I'd split the profits with him. He liked that idea.

As I thought about it, I wasn't sure what other projects were left for George to work on, but I think he was antsy to go on to something else anyway.

Or maybe he was still a little spooked from when we'd found the boys. He avoided talking about that. I never told him about Sara's ghost, and apparently, neither did Addie. That was probably for the best. I didn't want the whole town knowing about it; that could lead to issues and strange people sitting on the sidewalk at night, waiting to see something unworldly.

Meanwhile, Addie worked on cleaning up Sara's room. She got things done quicker than before because Marcie spent a lot of time next door. Lorraine decided that it was fun having a four-year-old to play with, especially one that you could send home whenever you felt like it. I never knew from one day to the next whether Marcie would be there or not when I got home.

The one big thing that remained open was the settlement from the insurance company. My lawyer had been going back and forth with them, and keeping me informed about the goings-on. The company had increased their offer, but Lawrence Railey, my lawyer, threatened to take them to court. Neither of us wanted that, but we were pretty sure the insurance company didn't want that either and would come up with a better offer.

So, it was no surprise when Lawrence called me at work. The insurance company had finally realized that this was a losing battle and that a court settlement was very likely to be much more than they really wanted to pay. This made perfect sense based on their client's history, but I wondered why it had taken them so long to figure it out. Maybe they had been waiting for me to get impatient and give in, but this was money I'd never expected to get anyway, so there had been no reason to hurry. Between selling the Chicago house and the money from Clara's accounts and IRAs, as well as what I had already saved over the years, I had no particular concerns as long as I kept my job.

I left the office and went over to Lawrence's office, only a couple of blocks away from mine. His receptionist showed me in and we exchanged pleasantries for a few minutes.

"Well, this hasn't been the easiest process to go through, Mr. Navelliere. For a while, I thought they were going to force us to go to court. That would have been a stupid thing for them to do, but you never know. Juries can be funny sometimes, but in this case, it looked to me like we held all the cards.

"They made an offer which is substantially larger than the prior one. But remember, the decision is entirely yours to make. We can take them to court if you want. I'll do whatever you say. And having said that, here is the offer they made." He handed me a piece of paper.

I looked over the paper carefully; it had only one number on it. My eyes opened in surprise. Even after Railey took his cut of it, I could probably retire just based on this if I wanted to. "Well, that is quite a jump from what they offered before." I thought for a moment. "What is your gut reaction?"

"I'd be very surprised if they will raise this. They know they will have a rough time of it, but if you don't want to accept this offer, I think we'll be going to court."

"And you think it's a fair offer?"

"Only you can answer that. Money is never going to replace your wife. The fact that you were in the process of getting a divorce also muddies the waters somewhat and I'm sure they'll use that against us. But her pregnancy is something that is highly likely to sway a jury. And with the prior DUI convictions for their client and the fact that his blood alcohol was way over the limit at the time of the accident, I think they know they are in trouble. Still, you never know when you go to a jury... they could award twice that, or half of it. It's pretty much a crap shoot, if you'll pardon my take on the justice system."

I thought about it a little longer while he watched me. "My initial reaction is to accept this offer. Part of me just wants to wrap up this hassle so I can move on. Another part of me wants to soak them for all that I can, just because their client is such an idiot."

"You don't have to decide now. Why don't you think about it for a few days and let me know?"

"Good idea. I'll get back to you in a day or two."

CHAPTER 43

I stopped by the lawyer's office two days later and accepted the settlement. A lot of paperwork needed to be filled out, but at least that wrapped it up. Lawrence told me it would take a couple of weeks for the check to come in, and that was fine with me.

As Lawrence walked me to the door, he stopped me for a moment. "Lou, I know how upset you were about this whole thing, so I didn't want to say anything until I was sure. I got word just before you got here that the driver that hit your wife was found guilty on several counts, including manslaughter. He'll be in jail a minimum of six months and lost his license for several years. Maybe that will give him time to think about what he's done."

"Well, he certainly deserves it. Some people never think about the damage they do until it is too late. While I hate to see someone go to jail, sometimes it seems like it's the only way to get through to them. I hope he uses this to turn himself around."

"Yeah, me too. I just thought you'd want to know."

"Thanks, Lawrence."

As I drove home, I thought about this turn of events. My life would be much easier with the insurance settlement, and his would be much harder with the time in jail, which probably meant he'd lose his job and who knows what else. Still, I couldn't help thinking about the baby daughter that I hadn't even known about.

So I felt conflicted when I walked in the door. I found Addie in the kitchen, sitting at the table thinking. "Something wrong, Addie?"

She gave me a small smile. "Kind of, but not really. I worked on Sara's room some more today. She had so many nice things and she was such a pretty girl. It's so sad what happened here."

I pulled up a chair and sat next to her. "I know what you mean. Once I got over the shock when I found out she was a ghost, I couldn't help but wonder what had brought on that sequence of events. She couldn't have done anything to deserve what she got. She was just so young and sweet, according to Drea."

She nodded. "You're right. I looked through the books and dolls and games in her room and then realized that in a few years Marcie will be her age. Sara had some nice things there, and it seemed like she would have had a lot of good memories. Did you see the paperweight on her nightstand?"

"The one from Disney World?"

She nodded.

"Yes, I saw that a couple of weeks ago. I'd been looking at it and when I looked up she stood by the door. Maybe there are some happy memories in there for her."

She was quiet for a few moments. "I don't know what I would do if something happened to Marcie."

"Well, I don't see anything like that happening again. At least not here. So I wouldn't worry about it if I were you."

"I guess you're right. I still have stuff to do and I should focus on that. Sara's room should be done in a day or two. What will you want me to do then?"

"Start all over again?"

She burst out laughing. "Well, if you really want me to. How come you always know how to make me laugh?"

I shook my head.

She smiled at me. "I think I'm going to move some of those wine bottles back into the basement now that George is finished down there. It looks much nicer than I expected."

"Are you doing that now?"

She nodded.

"Well, then I'll help. It's about time I did something useful around here."

We continued talking as we moved the bottles. We made a lot of trips from the third floor to the basement. "What did you tell Marcie about Sara?"

"Well, I took your suggestion. I was a little vague, but I told her that Sara would never be able to talk to her or play with her. I tried to explain the idea of a ghost, but I'm not really sure she understood. Maybe it's better that way."

"How did she react?"

"She didn't say too much. She was disappointed that Sara can't play with her. I think Marcie needs to hang out with kids her own age. I'm working on that. There are some kids in the family about her age, and I have some girlfriends with kids. I just need to get in contact with them."

"Well, if you need days off or whatever, let me know. You work too much anyway, and Marcie should be your first priority."

She smiled at me. "Thanks for saying that." Then she handed me another box of wine to carry.

CHAPTER 44

I wasn't particularly tired that night, so I spent some time in the library paying some of the bills that had piled up over the last week or so. Then I read for a while, but I felt restless and I went outside. It was a nice night, warm enough to be comfortable without a jacket, so I went through the conservatory and walked among the rose bushes. Kwan had done an excellent job with them and they were leafing out nicely. He'd replaced about a dozen or so that hadn't survived the years of neglect, but still, that was expected. Actually, it surprised me that he didn't find more to replace, and I looked forward to seeing them all in bloom.

After a few minutes, I headed back into the house, locking the door behind me. Lights were on in the kitchen, so I went there, figuring that Addie was still up. She sat at the kitchen table munching on cookies and reading a book. "Finally taking some time for yourself?"

She smiled but she looked tired. "I didn't want to read in the bedroom and keep Marcie awake, though sometimes I wonder if *anything* would wake her up. She sleeps very soundly, not like when she was a baby. Then it seemed like every little noise would wake her."

It was getting late, so I wished her a good night and went up the stairs after checking the front door locks. I turned left and went back to the boys' rooms. The drapes were open since it didn't make any difference and the light coming through the window lit up the rooms fairly well. Addie had done an excellent job of cleaning them up and they looked ready and waiting for someone to occupy them.

On a whim, I decided to check out Sara's room, which was almost done. With the lights off, I turned into the room and stopped, frozen. Sara was there. So was Harper. I went to move but he grabbed something off the nightstand and threw it...

CHAPTER 45

The next morning Addie came to the hospital to take me home. My head ached mercilessly even with all the drugs, but that was the least of my worries. They'd kept me overnight to make sure there was no concussion, which there wasn't, but they said to take it easy for a few days so I didn't fall again. I wasn't sure who had told them what, so I said nothing.

Addie was more concerned than I'd ever seen her, but she said almost nothing until we got in the car for her to drive us home. "Lou, I wasn't sure what to tell them last night. I heard a noise and when I went up to check you were lying on the floor in Sara's room, unconscious. At first I thought you just fell or something, but then I saw the paperweight lying on the floor next to you. I didn't know what happened. I called 911 right away and the ambulance got there a few minutes later. I didn't tell them anything other than what I saw and that it seemed like you fell."

I nodded, saying nothing.

"What *did* happen last night?"

I was more upset than I ever remembered. "I don't want to talk about it."

She said nothing more. When we pulled into the driveway, she tried to help me out of the car, but I shrugged her off and went inside and climbed the stairs to the library. A short while later she brought up a pot of coffee and some cups. "I wasn't sure what you wanted, but I thought this might help. That's an awfully big lump on your forehead."

I shook my head. "Bring me some Scotch."

She was startled. "Should you be having that with the medications?"

"Just bring it."

She brought it up to the library along with a glass and then left, probably afraid of what I'd say next.

So I poured some into the glass and drank it. Then I poured some more.

A while later I heard the doorbell ring, and shortly after that Sandi and Addie both came up.

"Nine-thirty in the morning is a little early for Scotch, don't you think?"

"No."

"You want to tell me what happened?"

I looked at her and said nothing.

Addie poured a cup of coffee for her after I declined again and poured myself more Scotch.

"Addie called me and said something bad happened last night and that you weren't talking to her and were drinking. She said something about a paperweight, but I don't understand."

I paused for only a moment. "He raped her."

I heard a gasp from Addie and turned to see her covering her mouth. "What? Who?"

"Harper."

"He raped his own daughter?"

I nodded, then looked back at Sandi, who sat there staring at me for a very long time. She took the extra empty coffee cup and poured herself some Scotch. Quietly, she said, "Tell me what happened."

Addie was pretty white by this time, but she had the sense to sit in a chair.

I looked at her. "Where's Marcie?"

"She spent the night with Drea. She's still over there."

I leaned back in the chair and took another drink. Somehow, it didn't taste like much of anything. It took a few moments to put my thoughts in order. "I wanted to look at Sara's room before I went to bed. I just wanted to see it cleaned up.

"When I walked through the door I saw them: Sara and Harper. She was crying and he was forcing himself on her. I was too shocked to do anything for a moment, but Harper saw me. He picked up something and threw it at me. The next thing I remember was waking up in the hospital."

Sandi stared at me for the longest time, then took another drink. "Are you sure of what you saw?"

I looked at her sideways. "Positive."

She looked down and shook her head. "You know, it's strange. For a long time, I didn't want to believe you when you said you saw Sara. But one piece of information was never released to the public, and only a few people in the department knew about it.

"We found evidence that she was molested and we ran DNA tests. We knew what he'd done, but kept it quiet. That was the only piece of information that could prove to me that this wasn't some hallucination. Sorry, but I guess I should have believed you from the start."

"Would it have made it easier?"

She shook her head. "Probably not."

I wiped the tears from my face and noticed that Addie was crying too, sitting there shocked.

"You know, Sandi, there is one thing that surprises me. No one really seemed to like Harper, but they all seemed to respect him. No one said anything that would have led me to guess this."

Sandi spoke up again. "I'm not sure what to tell you, Lou. Why this happened is way over my head."

I glanced at Addie again. "Yeah, ours too."

CHAPTER 46

I took the next week off from work and spent the first few days drunk. Addie looked in on me once in a while but mostly left me alone. I didn't blame her.

Eventually I realized that it wasn't helping, but I still had a hard time whenever I remembered what I'd seen and what had happened. Still, nothing I did would change it now, but I suspected that Sara was still around, though she hadn't reappeared.

Sandi came by on Wednesday to see how I was doing. "Still into the Scotch?"

"Not so much anymore. It didn't help, just made me numb."

She nodded. "Do you have a few minutes?"

"Sure, what do you need?"

"I just want to talk to you for a while. Let you know some of my thoughts ... things I couldn't say to you before."

"Sure, but we should have Addie join us, she's part of this discussion too."

Addie took her daughter next door for a while, then came back and joined us in the library. "Do we need Scotch for this discussion?"

I smiled. "I don't think so this time. Sergeant Johnson is here to officially interrogate us on what happened the other night."

She looked worried until Sandi said, "Well, no. I just want to talk. For your information, the department has no official position on ghosts. Mostly I want your thoughts on this, for me, personally and off the record, as a friend."

Addie relaxed at that and sat down with us.

"Seven years ago, when I went through the original investigation, we pieced together a lot of things. It wasn't difficult to figure out who'd committed the murders, but we found nothing to tell us why. And we wondered where the boys were. Then we got the autopsy and DNA reports on Sara and Harper and that told us a little more.

"So now we have a few more answers. We know the boys were killed, so we can at least wrap up that part. There was a lot of loose talk that somehow they'd gotten away, or had been kidnapped. At this point, though, it doesn't make a difference other than closing the loop. Have you come across anything that you haven't told me about?"

I shook my head. "Not really. I've pretty much told you everything that happened as we went along. Is there anything else you can't talk about?"

"Nope. If anything fit that category, I would at least tell you that. But the only piece we kept quiet was what Harper did to his daughter."

I thought out loud. "Well, if Stella somehow found out about that, it might have led to this whole thing."

Sandi nodded. "I wondered about that, too. She could have threatened to leave with the kids, or call the police, or whatever. That would have ruined Harper if it got out. What throws me, though, is that it didn't happen all at once. He let Drea go a few days before all of this with no real reason, just told her to get out."

Addie commented, "My family was very surprised when Drea was let go. Drea told us she could think of no reason why it happened. She thought maybe she did something wrong, but it was just her normal things—cleaning, cooking, and watching the kids."

Sandi nodded again. "There is nothing she did that would have led to this. She shouldn't even be thinking anything like that. I just hoped one of you had seen something else that would help."

"Abuse like that isn't the kind of thing that goes away," I offered. "Instead, it's likely to get worse."

"Well, that's true. And I think this is what triggered the whole thing to start with. As I think about it, it is the only thing that makes sense to me."

I looked at her. "I can't think of anything else that is relevant." I paused. "I don't think we will ever know for sure. All we can do is guess."

"Perhaps you're right."

I grinned at her. "I remember you saying your husband's grandmother talked about ghosts, maybe we could have her come over to help us out."

She grimaced. "Don't even think about it."

CHAPTER 47

I went back to work the following Monday and apologized to my boss. Since I'd just gotten out of the hospital, he told me to take it easy and not to worry about it. Actually, things in the office were going well. Even Roger was still behaving. Nevertheless, Ed was happy to have me back.

Railey, my lawyer, had tried to contact me a couple of times the prior week, but I had been in no shape to talk to anyone, so I finally returned his call. He had some more papers for me to sign and I told him I would stop by later in the day.

In the back of my mind, though, I still felt haunted by what I'd seen. I strongly suspected that I would see Sara again, and I wasn't sure how to handle it. The only one she consistently showed up for was me, so I guessed she was waiting for something from me. But what?

In reality, I got almost nothing done at work because I was so preoccupied, but no one noticed. I spent the day answering a few phone calls, sending emails, talking to people. They all expressed concern about my condition, but I just told them I'd tripped over something and hit my head on a piece of furniture ... really hard. That was close enough to the truth, and most of them said it was good that I was back. I still had swelling and bruising on my forehead, so it was pretty obvious.

I took off a little early that day, mostly to run by Railey's office. The papers were pretty much what I'd expected, so it only took about fifteen minutes. Then, as usual, I stopped by Marie's Flowers to pick up a white rosebud. For a change, Marie wasn't there, but she'd left instructions with her assistant, so it didn't take me long there either.

Then, with some trepidation, I went home. Odd, worrying about going home. It's the one place where most people feel safe. So had I until a week ago when I saw Sara and Harper. When would things be back to normal? Or would I have to face this as long as I lived there?

In one respect, it didn't matter. I wasn't leaving Rose House. I liked living here too much to do that. Besides, if the hauntings continued, I wouldn't be able to sell it anyway with a clear conscience.

When I got home, Addie had just finished cleaning the downstairs. Since she had done a major cleaning of the whole house once, now she settled into a weekly schedule, doing one floor a day, then working on other projects on the off days, like laundry and grocery shopping. Fortunately, this also gave her more time to spend with Marcie. This part of it almost started to seem normal. Was I getting spoiled? Well, yes, but I liked it.

Since she wasn't busy when I got there, I sat down in the kitchen to talk with her about what to do next with the house, but she wasn't very helpful. I suspected she was filled with ideas but felt reluctant to suggest spending my money. After a while I went up to the library to read, hoping it would put me in a better mood.

Somewhere in the middle of the book I was reading, I fell asleep. I had a nightmare with Harper beating Sara and it startled me awake, very upset. The room was too dim to continue reading and I was about to get up when I saw Sara. The dream came back to me, vividly.

She stood in the corner of the library, watching me, crying softly. Again she had a rosebud that she held near her face and she occasionally sniffed it.

I watched her for a minute or so, remembering everything that I knew about her. I felt the tears running down my cheeks.

"Sara, I'm so sorry for what happened to you. You were such a beautiful, sweet girl. Nothing like that should ever happen to a child. I wish I could change it."

Addie appeared in the doorway, about to say something. Then she apparently saw Sara, and just remained standing there.

"Sara, what happened to you was a horrible, horrible thing. I can't understand why anyone would do that, least of all your father. I am so sorry. I don't know what to say or how to make it up to you."

She stood there, watching, and listening. Once in a while, she would glance over at Addie, but then she turned back to me.

"Sara, is there anything I can do? If you can tell me, I'll do it." I wiped some more tears from my face and watched her.

And she disappeared.

Addie turned to me and spoke quietly. "You know, Lou, you're one of the nicest people I've ever met. I wasn't sure if I should come here looking for a job, but now I'm so glad I did. I would never have suspected that someone could come to care that much about a ghost."

I shook my head and stood up, and we walked downstairs to dinner.

CHAPTER 48

The next few days were normal again. No visits from Sara, just my job and the routine of the household. I called Sandi to let her know Sara showed up again, but she was in the middle of a case and couldn't make it by for a few days.

She showed up on Thursday evening after dinner. At the time, Marcie was in the master bedroom playing with Furball, who of course loved the attention until he didn't. So we left her there and went into the library. I sat behind the desk, my usual place, and she sat across from me. Addie showed up moments later with some Scotch and glasses and poured some for each of us.

I looked over at her. "Will Marcie be okay where she is?"

She nodded. "I think so. She won't be able to hear us and I'm close if she needs something."

I went over the events from the last Sara appearance with her. There wasn't much to tell, only that she'd showed up and I'd talked to her. It's not like she had told me anything.

Her eyes moved from Addie to me. "Any ideas come to you about what she wants?"

"Not really. Unless there is a piece missing here that we haven't found, I don't know what she could want."

She shook her head. "That would surprise me. This case has been rolling around in the back of my head for seven years now. The obvious piece was the missing boys, but that's resolved. The other piece that we knew was what Harper did to her, but that wasn't public knowledge. And I don't see any way we'll ever know definitely what the reasons were.

"But maybe you're making too much of this. You haven't seen her for a few days. Maybe all she wanted was for someone to know what happened. And on top of that, you apologized to her for what was done. She hasn't been here for a few days; maybe that was enough."

"Well, that would be nice, I suppose. But she never had a pattern to when she did and didn't appear. How would I even know if she was gone? She could show up again a year from now."

"I don't know, Lou. I probably shouldn't say this, but you knew what you were getting into when you bought this house. Maybe she just wants to keep you company, or wants someone to keep her company and not forget her."

"I could never forget her, no matter what happened."

At a pause in the conversation, a very serious Marcie showed up at the door. She walked slowly into the room. Then we saw Sara behind her, followed by a woman. It took me a moment to place her.

Stella, her mother.

I glanced over at Sandi. She sat there perfectly still, staring. I guessed she could see them also. Addie too just watched.

Marcie went over to Addie and climbed into her lap. The girl still hadn't said a word, but just looked at Sara.

I looked back towards Sara and her mother. Slowly, the little blond girl walked over to the desk and placed her rose on it, in front of me. Then she walked back to her mother and turned around to face me. Stella put a hand on her daughter's shoulder. I'll never forget the last I saw of her: she looked over at me and, for the very first time, I saw Sara smile.

CHAPTER 49

The following several days were normal, with one exception. I still brought in a rose every day and Addie put it in a vase, but they stopped disappearing. Each day I threw out the old one and put the new one in its place. I continued this for a couple of weeks.

Addie asked me about it one morning.

"Well, I think Sara is gone, but I just want to be sure. You know how obsessive I am."

She smiled and nodded.

On Saturday morning, as I walked out the door to go to Marie's, Sandi showed up.

"So, Sandi, are you going to stop bugging your husband's grandmother about ghosts?"

"I will never say anything against her again. I still can't believe it.'

For a moment I was serious. "After all this, I'm glad that you got to see Sara."

"Yeah, me too."

"Did you need anything in particular?"

"No, I was in the neighborhood and wanted to check in on you. Looks like you are heading out."

"I was going to Marie's for flowers."

"Are they still disappearing?"

"No, that stopped after we saw Sara the last time. I think she's gone."

"You need a ride down there? I'm not in the middle of anything."

"Sure."

Oddly, we said almost nothing on the drive, preoccupied with our own thoughts.

She raised her eyebrows when I got back into the car with my order, but asked no questions, just drove me home.

I walked into the kitchen where Addie was cleaning up. She looked at me, surprised. "A box? You got a dozen roses for Sara?" She opened them up. They were red. She looked confused. "What?"

"They're for you, Addie."

A host of emotions played across her face for a moment. Then her eyes opened wide and she threw her arms around my neck.

I wanted to say something else to her, but her lips were far too interesting.

I heard a noise behind me.

"Mommy's got a boyfriend!"

END

ROSE HOUSE

ABOUT THE AUTHOR

Robert Crandall was born and raised in Saint Louis, Missouri, where he graduated from Washington University. He worked in Information Systems before turning to fiction (those two may be related, or even the same). Currently, he resides in a quiet western Saint Louis suburb and prefers to drink single malt Scotch.

Note from the author: Thank you for reading this book. As an independent writer, reviews can be very important, so if you enjoyed this book, please leave a review on your favorite book website. Thanks again!

Made in the USA
Columbia, SC
19 July 2019